# Kids on the Run

# Barbara Mitchelhill

Andersen Press • London

*For a real live Max and his brother Tom*

First published in 2005 by
Andersen Press Limited,
20 Vauxhall Bridge Road, London SWIV 2SA
www.andersenpress.co.uk

The right of Barbara Mitchelhill to be identified as the author of
this work has been asserted by her in accordance with the
Copyright, Designs and Patents Act, 1988

British Library Cataloguing in Publication Data available

ISBN 1 84270 388 9

Typeset by FiSH Books, London WC1
Printed and bound in Great Britain by Bookmarque Ltd.,
Croydon, Surrey

# Chapter 1

I've been thinking about the difference between real life and programmes on the telly – 'Superman' or a cops series or spy films. If you ask me, the difference is that the telly is dead exciting. Real life is boring – most of the time anyway.

Mine was mega yawn-making until a few months ago. Then everything changed when I got involved in a diamond robbery. That livened it up, I can tell you! Goodbye boredom. Hello danger and run-for-your-life.

Of course, it didn't happen all of a sudden. There were things leading up to it – like Dad losing his job.

OK. Maybe I should have been more sympathetic when he told me. Maybe I should have said, 'Bad luck, Dad,' or 'Never mind, Dad,' or 'Something will turn up, Dad.' But I didn't. I was watching a video at the time and it was just getting to the good bit where the vampire was plunging his fangs into the girl's neck and the hero was trying to smash down the door.

'Did you hear what I said, Max?' Dad said. 'Can't you take your eyes off the television? I'VE LOST MY JOB.'

It was obvious he was expecting a reply so I said, 'No job is cool, Dad. You'll have time to take us fishing.'

It seemed a reasonable suggestion – but Dad couldn't see it. Not even when I pointed out all the other things he could do now he didn't have to work from nine to five.

'Take a break, Dad,' I said. 'Life's too short.'

His face (usually really pale) suddenly turned pink. Almost purple. It was probably high blood pressure or something. I think he should see a doctor.

'Take a break? What are you talking about, Max. I've lost my job!'

I tried to keep him calm. But he didn't. I told him to look on the bright side. But he just got worse.

'Stop it, Max,' said Kaz, who's my sister and a bit of a pain. 'Can't you see Dad's upset?'

What did she know? Nothing, that's what.

She told me to grow up.

I told her to get real.

She said I was a pain in the neck.

I said she was a pain in the bum.

She said I was stupid.

I said she had a brain the size of a pea.

For some reason, Dad suddenly lost his temper. 'Don't you two understand?' he yelled.

'What?' I said.

'What?' said Kaz.

'If I don't have a job,' he said, 'I won't have a wage.'

We knew that.

'There'll be no pocket money, Max.'

'You mean . . .'

'No pocket money. No goodies. No treats.'

I hadn't thought about it quite like that, so it was a bit of a shock.

'But what about my new football strip, Dad?'

He made a funny gurgling noise in his throat and ground his teeth together.

'I'll take that as a "no", shall I?' I said.

I don't suppose a grown-up can imagine how depressing news like that can be for a kid. It could mean the collapse of my football career. I needed the proper gear for the County Football Final. My shorts were torn in two places. The shirt was almost as bad. How serious is that?

Kaz nudged me. 'Don't be selfish, Max,' she said. 'Dad promised me some new jeans last week. I'm going out on Saturday, remember.'

A spotty oaf called Jason was taking my sister to the pictures. I don't know why. She's no fun. She's only interested in clothes.

Anyway, Dad told her she couldn't have the jeans. 'Sorry, Kaz,' he said. 'Unless I get a job, I'm skint.'

What did she do? She burst into tears and ran out of the room in one of her moods. Typical!

After that, things got even worse.

'It's desperate at home,' I told my mate, Jamie. 'No beefburgers or crisps now. No chocolate. I can feel myself fading away.' And to demonstrate, I flexed my arms to show my withering muscles.

Luckily, Jamie told his mum (who is an awesome cook), and she invited me round for tea. She could probably see how thin I was getting. Jamie was dead lucky to have a mum like her. In fact, I was working on a cunning plan so my dad could meet her. I knew he'd

3

think she was fantastic. She has terrific blue eyes and curly blonde hair. My idea was that they could get together and Jamie and me could be one family (with good food).

I went round for tea loads of times – my favourite meal was steak pie and chips. Even after three weeks, things at home were no better. Dad still hadn't found a job.

One afternoon as I was finishing my apple crumble, Jamie's mum noticed I was feeling really bad. I always tried to hide my troubles, but it was difficult.

'What's the matter, Max?' she said. 'You don't look your usual cheerful self.'

She was right. How could I look cheerful when I had serious money problems?

'I'm broke,' I said and told her the whole truth about the football gear. 'So if I don't get the money, I'll be playing in the Final with holes in my shorts.'

She came up with a great solution. 'A car boot sale,' she said. 'There's one at the school on Saturday. You could sell your old toys and things that you don't need any more.'

I was impressed. What an amazing mum! She could probably solve the problems of the world if she wanted to. I was more convinced than ever that she was the right person for my dad. I would get working on the MY DAD AND JAMIE'S MUM PROJECT as soon as possible.

For the time being, the Car Boot Project was top of the list. I went home and spent ages sorting out games and comics. A whole cardboard boxful! I even found a jumper Auntie Jean knitted me (I never liked it) and a few old clothes from Kaz's wardrobe. Some were quite scruffy. But I thought somebody might buy them.

The Car Boot Sale was a great opportunity to make loads of money – so I had to think big. Would toys and old clothes be enough? Maybe not. Maybe I should think of something else.

So I came up with...PLANTS!

Plants were dead popular at car boot sales. I even knew where I could find some – for free. Just down the road from our house was the town park and there were loads of them there. Only last week, I'd seen the gardeners planting hundreds – no thousands – of flowers in the beds so they spelled TOWN CENTENARY. Dead clever! But they were so tightly packed together that they were almost choking to death. They needed space to grow and I was sure that no one would notice if I took a few. See? A brilliant but simple idea.

This was how I did it:

Step 1: Our next-door neighbour, Mrs Roberts, kept loads of empty pots in her back garden. I don't know why. She never used them. So I made a small hole in the fence, pushed my hand through and borrowed about twenty.

Step 2: I pulled my plastic sledge off the top shelf in the shed where Dad keeps tins of paint. A bit messy, but I did it. Then I put the pots on the sledge and pulled them down to the park.

Step 3: When nobody was around, I dug up a few

5

plants from the bed – a pink one here, a red one there – and put them in the pots. A big hairy dog came over and dug up a few more than I intended. Never mind.

Step 4: I dragged the plants home – followed by the dog – and hid them in the shed. I knew they would sell for a fortune.

That night, I felt really pleased with myself. My new football strip was in sight. My short-term money problem was solved. The snag was that, once that money was gone, we would still be dead poor. I had to think of some way of making money Big Time.

I sat up in bed and I made a list.

1 Rob a bank. (Will probably get spotted on CCTV.)
2 Join a pop group. (Can't sing. Can't play an instrument.)
3 Be a famous footballer. (Not old enough to play in major team yet.)
4 Write a book.

The last one sounded good. Writers made loads of money and Dad would never have to go out to work again and we could have really good food and I'd be famous (like J. K. Rowling). I decided to start writing that night and hope I'd finish the book by the end of next week. Even if the publisher was dead slow, I would expect to be earning millions when the book started to sell in a month or so. Right! That was a superb long-term strategy.

I pulled a notebook out of a drawer and wrote the first chapter before I fell asleep.

# REDWON THE WONDER BOY
## CHAPTER 1

There was once a boy called Redwon. A weird name. But for someone with sisters called Blootwo and Greenthree, it wasn't very surprising. He came from an ordinary family of superheroes. At least his father was a superhero. His mother didn't go in for that kind of thing. She concentrated on steak pies in order to keep Dad's strength up.

One day, Redwon's superhero dad ran into a spot of trouble. In fact, he was killed. This was owing to a bad cold which seriously decreased his powers while he was fighting the Black Serpents (they were very common in those parts). He was definitely dead.

'That's it!' said Redwon's mum who was in a really bad mood. 'I've had enough. You are the last remaining male in our family, Redwon. If I keep you here, those Black Serpents will get you too. And I won't have it!'

There wasn't much point in her talking to Redwon as he was only two months old. But it's the thought that counts.

Struggling for miles with three babies on her back, she found a wood and left Redwon under a bush.

'I'll be in touch,' she said and, with tears

dripping off the end of her nose, she tucked his favourite teddy under his little arm.

What with the tears and the wet grass, Redwon was rather damp. So it was lucky that a man came into the wood looking for mushrooms. This was a dangerous occupation as the man was short-sighted and could never be sure which were mushrooms and which were toadstools. He was just heading towards a new spot when he tripped over Redwon and fell flat on his face.

'What's that?' he said to himself. It was obvious to anyone that it was a baby because it was crying loud enough to be heard for at least ten miles.

He fumbled around until he found little Redwon under some dock leaves and he picked him up. Although the man was poor, he was very kind and he took the baby home.

He didn't know the baby's real name, of course, and he decided to call him Watt. (When he found him, he had said, 'What's that?' so it seemed like a good name.) From then on – at least when he could talk – Watt called the man Dad.

Watt's new dad was so poor that he wore only rags thrown out by the charity shop and a pair of second-hand glasses. They often went hungry, except in the mushroom season, and life was hard.

Year after year went by with nothing much

happening until the day of Watt's tenth birthday. Then his mother appeared in a dream.

'My son,' she said, 'I know it's been a long time but I've been really busy. Now you're ten, I thought I'd better tell you that you are no ordinary boy. Your real name is Redwon.'

'That's a stupid name,' said Watt.

'No more stupid than Watt,' she said, in a bit of a temper. 'Redwon is wonder spelled backwards.'

'I'm not good at spelling backwards.'

'Take it from me. It spells wonder.'*

'Wonder what?' said Redwon.

'Not what,' said his mother. 'You are a wonder. You are special and brave and strong and you have magical powers.'

This was a bit of a shock on a Monday morning. But, after the dream, when Watt woke up, he found that his mother had left him a cloak with a label which said '50% wool, 50% magic. Dry-clean only.'

Watt was well impressed and slipped it over his shoulders.

'Nice colour,' he said as he stood in front of the mirror. Then, to his amazement, he began to change. He stared and watched as he turned

---

*Those of you who have checked this out will notice that Redwon's mum was not as good at spelling backwards as she thought.

into a superhero – the amazing Redwon – and a large red R appeared on his forehead.

Suddenly, sparkly things appeared before his eyes and, as they cleared, he realised that he could see for miles. The true laser eyesight of the superhero.

His hearing improved as well. This was particularly useful as it had never been very good owing to poor attention to washing. Now he could hear amazing things – a worm cough, a snail snore, a blackbird laugh.

Not only that – he soon discovered that he could fly like a jet plane.

'That's cool!' he said. 'I'll go and find riches so that Dad won't starve any more.' And he zoomed off over the hills and valleys searching for any jewels and gold that might be lying around.

Eventually, he came to a steep cliff with steps cut in the sides. 'Course, he didn't need the steps, he just zotted over the edge right down to a cave which looked very interesting. Once in the cave, he found that twisting passageways went deep into the hillside. Anyone else would have been dead scared. But not Redwon. He went right inside until the passages opened out into a cavern and there he found a large wooden box marked THE JEWELS OF JAYBAL – DO NOT REMOVE. ANYONE FOUND STEALING THIS WILL BE HUNG, DRAWN AND QUARTERED OR KILLED.

'This is my lucky day,' said Redwon (Watt) who never read small print. Instead, he opened the box and saw the most amazing thing – a gold football studded with diamonds and rubies. It belonged to the King of Jaybal who had once played goalkeeper for United and it was worth a fortune.

'Dad will be pleased,' said Redwon (Watt). 'I'll sell this and we'll be dead rich.'

But things didn't work out as well as he thought they would.

# Chapter 2

The Boot Sale was going to be dead exciting. Jamie was going to help, so he came round early on Saturday morning.

'We'll get the best pitch and make loads of money,' I said as we set off with all our stuff.

But things didn't go smoothly at first. There was this man sitting behind a table at the gate. Really mean looking, he was.

'Five pounds, lads,' he said holding out his hand. I was shocked. Five pounds?

'I haven't got five pounds,' I said.

'No money, no pitch,' he said. 'That's the rule.'

I looked at Jamie then I put on my 'starving orphan boy' look and turned back to the man.

'I haven't got any money at all,' I said in a quaking voice. 'That's why I'm selling my toys.'

Nobody could resist my big tearful eyes and my drooping shoulders. He was no exception. (I might be an actor when I grow up – when I get bored with being a famous writer.)

'I'll tell you what,' he said. 'Pay me out of your earnings when you've finished.' Then he winked. 'Only don't tell anybody else or they'll all think they can do it.'

Bingo! We set up our pitch and waited for the customers to come.

I managed to sell Kaz's stuff straight away – that was a surprise! Even my jumper sold and the plants, too. Then nothing happened for hours until a kid offered me five pence for all my comics. It was an insult. I'd had those comics for years. But I gave in and took the money.

In the end, after all the work, I'd only made £7.45.

'Come on,' I said to Jamie. 'Let's go home.' I was fed up, I can tell you.

We packed up and were walking towards the gate, when a someone shouted, 'Oy!' It was the man at the table, expecting his money. Five pounds out of our takings! No way!

We legged it across the field. 'Oy! You two,' he yelled again. 'Come back!' But we were well clear of the fence before he could catch up with us, owing to him being overweight and breathless. Maybe after that experience he will see how important it is to keep fit.

Unfortunately, the next day there was a bit of a problem.

Kaz didn't seem to appreciate that I had cleared out the rubbish from her wardrobe. When she saw some stuff was missing, she freaked out. I couldn't understand it myself. I was doing her a favour.

'You've got to tell him, Dad,' she moaned. 'He bursts into my bedroom. He takes my clothes to the car boot. They were designer stuff from the market! Now what can I wear? I've got nothing decent. Honestly, my life isn't worth living.' And she turned on the tears – again.

Then Mrs Roberts from next door came round complaining about her missing plant pots.

'I save those and wash 'em and stack 'em neatly till the winter. Now they're gone. Except for the ones that got broken.'

I couldn't see what she was on about. She never used them.

'And what's more,' she said, 'there's a hole in the fence. Now who's done that, that's what I want to know?'

Dad wasn't pleased. He had a right go at me and made me apologise and clean her patio slabs until they were spotless. It was very hard work. He repaired the hole – even though I didn't think that was necessary. The hole was only small. Worst of all, I had to give up my £7.45 to Kaz. Doom!

That evening, I flopped in the armchair, exhausted. The local news was on. Bad news for me when I heard the first item.

'Judges for the Parks in Bloom Competition arrived at the park yesterday morning, only to find that vandals had been at work and removed some of the plants,' the newsreader announced. I sat up and listened.

There were shots of the park. I thought they looked quite nice. Very bright and cheerful.

'The Parks Department had been hoping to win the cup for their special flower display,' the newsreader continued.

Another shot of the park. Another flowerbed.

'This display should have read TOWN CENTENARY, but after the theft, it was left with the words  OWN CENT  NARY. The police are determined they will catch whoever is responsible.'

So the police were looking for me. This was depressing news for a kid who was only trying to earn an honest living.

I went up to my room to continue my novel.

# CHAPTER 2

When Redwon reached home, he quickly turned back into Watt – although he had a problem with the R on his forehead and had to spit on a tissue and rub quite hard before it disappeared. He was dying to show his dad the Jewels of Jaybal but it was Friday and Dad was doing overtime in the mine at the other end of town.

While Watt waited, he rustled up a pan of mushroom soup. (He was a brilliant cook and hoped to have his own TV show one day.)

While the soup was bubbling, he switched on the radio he had recently made using spare parts from an old washing machine. He was hoping for a bit of pop music but it was the news. The news was usually dead boring – but not today. Somebody was interviewing the Chief of the Black Serpents. (You'll remember that Watt's superhero dad had been killed by one.) The Black Serpents were mega vicious. Half-men, half-monsters with stinking breath who terrified people for miles around.

'So how long have the Jewels of Jaybal been missing?' the interviewer asked – and Watt pricked up his ears as the Jewels were currently sitting on the kitchen table.

'Not long,' said the Chief in a low gravelly voice which was seriously spooky. 'They have been stolen and I am here to tell you all that we will search and find whoever has taken them.'

'Any idea who that might be?'

'Oh yes. We think we know the scummy little thief.'

'Then what?'

'DEATH.'

Watt couldn't stop shaking. Even jamming his fist in his mouth couldn't stop it. He knew that the Black Serpents boiled their captives in pots over roaring fires, only pausing to add salt and pepper and a few mixed herbs.

There was nothing for Watt to do except to hide the Jewels somewhere and hope that the Black Serpents would not think of looking in the wood.

I'd just finished the second chapter, when I heard a car pull up outside our house. I looked out of the window and there was a bloke in a dark suit climbing out of a flash red car – tinted windows and everything. It was dead embarrassing that his car was parked next to Dad's old rust bucket. Anyway, this guy walked up to our front door smoking a big fat cigar.

Dad let him in and I was dying to know who he was,

so I pressed my ear to the floor – but I couldn't hear a thing. He left after ten minutes and I went back to the window. Guess what? I saw him climbing into a taxi and off he went, leaving his cool machine behind.

'What's happening, Dad?' I said as I dashed downstairs. 'Why did that man leave his car?'

Dad grinned. 'It's mine, Max,' he said, slapping me on the shoulder. 'Dean Holland gave me a loan to buy it.'

'Cor!' I was dead impressed. 'Was that Dean Holland then?'

'Yes. That was him. I've got a job working as his chauffeur. That's the deal.'

'He must be mega rich to have his own chauffeur.'

'Well,' said Dad. 'I won't be driving him all the time. I'll have my own taxi service. I'll have to work hard to pay back the money but at least I'll have a job.'

'Does that mean I get my pocket money now?'

'Not for a while, son.'

No change then.

Dad told us he was going to start work the next day.

'I'll be working evenings as well as daytime,' he said.

Kaz didn't like it at all. 'You can't be serious, Dad! I'm not staying in every night to babysit my horrible little brother. How will I ever have any social life?'

Then they argued.

Dad said she was being selfish.

Kaz said she'd never see her friends.

Dad said he had to pay back the loan.

Kaz said she'd die an old maid.

18

Dad said she was being dramatic.

Then she burst into tears and ran up to her room. So what's new?

Me? I stayed cool and switched on the telly.

# Chapter 3

A few days after Dad started his new job, Jamie (my very best mate in all the world) dropped a bombshell that ruined my carefully thought-out plans for the future.

'Mum and me are moving in with Craig,' he told me. 'You know Craig. He's the one with the brilliant sports car.'

I felt really upset and angry – all at the same time.

'I know who Craig is,' I said, grinding my teeth. 'But what d'you mean? Moving in.'

'Mum said it would be great for us to live in the same house. She asked me if I minded and I said it was OK.'

I could hardly believe it! He said it was OK! How could he let me down like that? How could he encourage his mum to live with anyone other than my dad? This was depressingly bad news.

'You've ruined our plans, Jamie. And what about the football team? I suppose you'll be quitting that.'

Jamie laughed. ''Course not. I'm still in the team. Craig's even bought me a new strip for the Final . . . and boots. I'll bring 'em round to show you later.'

'You mean you'll still be going to our school?'

'Yeah. Craig lives in Hanover Road. It's not far.'

'That's dead posh. Does he live in one of those big houses?'

'Yeah. Loads of bedrooms and I think he's got a jacuzzi.'

'Cor!'

'Bunk beds as well. You can come and stay anytime you want.'

'Brilliant!'

Maybe things weren't quite as bad as I thought.

Thinking about it, my main problem was this: there were only ten days to the Final and I was broke. My novel wasn't likely to be in the shops before then – so how could I get the money to replace my embarrassing gear?

I thought about it all day but, before I could think of a solution, Dad came home from work. He was really tired and definitely needed something to cheer him up. So I told him this brilliant joke about the cow with three legs. It had gone down a storm with the kids in our class. When I told Dad, he didn't even smile.

'I'm sorry, Max. I'm shattered,' was all he said. 'I've driven Dean Holland all over London and then on to Heathrow. Nothing went right. He kept saying, "Put your foot down. Can't you drive faster?" I tell you, we nearly had a crash on the way.'

He'd had a rotten day. Maybe a different joke would make him feel better. But I couldn't get a word in.

'The traffic was terrible and Dean's temper was worse. He nearly missed his plane. He jumped out of the car almost before I'd stopped and he dashed into the airport without so much as a thank you.'

Our dad slumped back in his chair and pressed his fingers over his eyes. He looked worn out.

'Go and have a bath, Dad,' I said in my best considerate-son voice. 'It'll make you feel good.'

I had suddenly thought up a cunning plan to solve my financial problem. While Dad was relaxing in the bath, I would clean and polish his car. When he came down – BINGO! Spotless, brand new, shiny, sparkly car. 'Oh Max!' he'd say. 'You must have worked so hard. What a marvellous son you are!' He'd be so grateful, he'd offer to buy the football strip. Brilliant, eh?

It took me ages to do the car. At least fifteen minutes. Soap and water first, then a rub down with a duster. I picked up loads of rubbish from inside as well as a pair of glasses, a black bag, and a thermos flask. I was carrying them into the house when Jamie arrived.

'What d'you think about the car?' I said. 'Doesn't it look great, eh?'

'Amazing!' he said and we walked inside. 'Now see what I've got.' He dumped a brand new sports bag on the table and pulled out his new strip and the boots.

I was impressed. 'Try them on, Jamie, and we'll have a practice out the back.'

'I can't. Craig's waiting. We're just on our way to the travel agents.'

'What for?'

'To book a trip to EuroDisney. Cool, eh?'

'Yeah, cool,' I said. I felt deeply depressed.

'Maybe you could come with us,' said Jamie. 'Craig

likes you, you know. Remember when you told him one of your jokes and he really laughed.'

That cheered me up a bit.

'If I tell him some more, maybe he'll invite me. What do you think? How about the one about the cow with three legs?'

'Good choice! That'll win him over. No problem.'

We were deep into planning our trip when Craig beeped his horn.

'Gotta go,' Jamie said and he grabbed his bag and raced out. 'See yer!'

I felt quite cheerful after that. Dad was still in the bath, relaxing, so I'd got time to clear away the stuff from the car. I took the pile off the table where I'd dumped it, put the rubbish in the bin and took the rest upstairs to his bedroom.

Meanwhile, I put a 'Star Trek' video on and put my feet up on the sofa. I was exhausted after cleaning the car.

Then the phone went.

Kaz dashed in from the kitchen. 'I'll get it! I'll get it!' she said. 'It'll be Jason.'

But I raced her to it and snatched up the receiver.

'Max!' she whined.

Anyway, it wasn't Jason. It was Dean Holland for Dad. The line wasn't all that clear. Pretty fuzzy, actually.

'Hang on,' I said. 'I'll go and get him.'

I shouted upstairs. 'Dad! Phone!' but he couldn't hear and I had to go and hammer on the bathroom door.

'Dad! It's Dean Holland. He wants to talk to you – urgent, he said.'

Dad came shooting out of the bathroom, covered in soap, with a towel round his middle.

I went back to watch 'Star Trek' but Dad was talking in a really loud voice, so I had to turn the volume up. He kept saying, 'No, I haven't seen it.' and 'Definitely not.' and 'I'm certain.' Then he dropped the phone on the table and dashed outside. You should have seen him – half-naked outside in our road, diving into his car! Mrs Roberts next door was clipping her hedge at the time and she nearly passed out. What a laugh!

He wasn't long. He was soon back on the phone talking to Dean Holland – which was a bit annoying, as it was hard to concentrate on what Jean-Luc Picard was saying to Data.

Anyway, after that, Dad was in a real mood. He sat in his chair biting his lip. Then he got up and paced backwards and forwards. There was something wrong. But I didn't know what. Was this the time to point out that I'd been cleaning his car all afternoon? I decided to play it cool and wait until the morning.

'Aren't you working tonight, Dad?' Kaz asked later on.

'No,' he said. 'I'm expecting someone round. I don't know what time they'll come.'

'Then I'm off for an early night,' she said. 'Jason's taking me to the pictures tomorrow.'

I knew she wasn't going to bed. I saw her pick up Dad's mobile as she walked behind the sofa. She'd spend ages talking to lover-boy – who must be seriously lacking in the brains department to want to go out with my sister.

I stretched my arms above my head and gave a massive yawn. 'I'm whacked,' I said. 'I think I'll get an early night, too.'

This was the perfect opportunity to write chapter 3.

# CHAPTER 3

Well, the Black Serpents didn't come looking for the Jewels that day, but something terrible happened all the same. The mine where Watt's dad worked collapsed. This was because Owen, the foreman, had a shocking memory and left sticks of dynamite lying around. These had a nasty habit of blowing up when least expected.

That was exactly what happened that morning. BOOM! went the dynamite. CRASH! the roof of the mine.

Watt heard about the accident on the radio. 'I'd better get moving,' he said and he grabbed his cloak and an old crash helmet to protect his head from falling rocks. In a flash, he had changed into Redwon, superhero, and jetted to the far side of town. When he arrived at the mine, there was nothing left – only a great pile of rubble. The entrance had collapsed and there was no way in.

'Oh, panic, panic!' cried Owen, the foreman.

'No hope. No hope,' sobbed the Chief Engineer.

But Redwon had other ideas.

'Stand back!' he shouted.

Then, with the strength of a guided missile, he dived into the rubble. Although he had a problem with his crash helmet slipping over his eyes, he still managed to spot his dad's feet sticking out from under a massive boulder.

'Hold on!' he called. 'I'll save you.'

The superhero managed to roll back the boulder and pull him to safety.

Unfortunately, his father's legs had been rolled flat as pastry and were now twice as long as they had been.

'Thanks for saving me,' said Dad as he lay all floppy on the ground. 'But who are you? What's your name?'

Redwon smiled and said, 'You're right.'

But his dad didn't see the joke. (Watt's your name? – good, eh?)

So the superhero laid his hand on his father's shoulder and said, 'Goodbye for now, old man.'

The Chief Engineer took Dad home on a flat-bed trailer as he was now too long to fit inside a normal car. When he arrived, Redwon had changed back to Watt, of course, and was busy adding a few handfuls of grass to the soup for a bit of colour.

'I'm home, son,' Dad called.

Watt went over to the door. 'You've changed, Dad,' he said and carried him to the fire, arranging his amazing long thin legs on the hearth.

'I know,' said Dad. 'I'll never be able to work in the mine again.'

'A circus, maybe?' Watt suggested helpfully. But there wasn't a circus for miles.

'I'm redundant,' Dad said. 'We'll need a miracle to save us. If only the superhero would come back to help.'

I finished the last sentence and shut my book, when there was a loud knock at the front door. Dad's visitors, I thought. But, when I looked out of the window, I saw a police car parked outside our house.

Oh no! They must have come for me. They must have found evidence to link me to the Town Park Flower Robbery. I felt sick – like at the fair when you've had greasy chips then go on the Big Dipper.

I closed my eyes and waited. Any minute now, I would be arrested, fitted with handcuffs and taken off to prison.

# Chapter 4

As it turned out, it wasn't me the police wanted. They had come to talk to Dad.

I went down to Kaz's room, ignoring the notice KEEP OUT! ESPECIALLY MAX and poked my head round the door. She was lying on the bed, her face covered in white concrete stuff.

'Max! I thought I told you…' she yelled. But when she opened her mouth, the concrete stuff cracked into little pieces. What a joke! But she couldn't see the funny side.

'You've ruined my face pack,' she screamed, 'and I've got a date tomorrow!' Then she threw a book at me.

'All right,' I said, 'so I won't tell you the police are here.'

My sister is so predictable. She leaped off the bed and we both went to the top of the stairs so we could hear what was going on. We thought it might be about a speeding ticket or a witness to a mobile snatch. Something like that.

But we were wrong.

We heard every word – and we were gobsmacked! They were on about a robbery in Hatton Garden.

'What's Hatton Garden?' I whispered to Kaz.

'Where they buy and sell diamonds.'

'Wow! Fantastic!' I said. 'A diamond robbery!'

I thought they only had those in cop shows on telly. I'd never known of one near us.

'It's a joke,' Kaz whispered. 'It must be. Why do they want to talk to Dad about it?'

I nodded. The Old Bill had made a boo-boo.

But it didn't sound like a joke for Dad. I could tell that. He was getting really mad. His voice was getting louder. Then there was a bit of a scuffle and a bump or two and policemen's voices.

'Now then, sir!'

'Hey up!'

'Are you threatening us, sir?'

After some angry words, one of the policemen finally said in a very deep serious voice, 'Mark Westall, I am arresting you on conspiracy to...'

Kaz didn't wait for them to finish. She let out a scream and raced downstairs – which must have been really scary for the police, seeing our Kaz with bits of white concrete on her face looking like a banshee.

'No!' she yelled. 'Stop it! You can't take my dad. You can't. What do you mean, trying to arrest him?'

She was hysterical. Like a wild cat. I stayed well away at the top of the stairs. I didn't want the police to see me. They might recognise me and decide to arrest me in connection with the Town Park Flower Robbery.

Kaz kept on wailing while Dad tried to calm her down. 'OK, OK, Kaz. I'll sort it out, sweetheart,' he said, 'I've got to go with the police but I'll be back soon.'

Kaz sniffled.

30

'When I've gone,' said Dad, 'I want you to lock up and go to bed. Don't answer the door if anyone calls. I'll be here when you and Max wake up in the morning.'

You see, I knew it was a mistake and Dad knew it was a mistake.

Then one of the policemen spoke to Kaz, 'Will you be all right by yourself, young lady, or shall we contact Social Services?'

I could imagine Kaz's face, all white and flaky and angry. I bet she was on the verge of thumping him.

'I'm not a child!' she snapped. 'I'm old enough to look after my little brother. You may be taking his dad away but he's still got me! Or are you thinking or arresting me, as well?'

Good old Kaz! It was a great put-down. I bet the police had red faces after that!

'Right-o, miss,' said Plod. 'We'll be off then.'

Once they'd walked out and I'd heard the door slam shut, I raced down to Kaz.

'Cor! They've really arrested him! Did he get hand-cuffed?'

'Yes,' Kaz said.

'Wow! I wish I'd seen it. I've only ever seen handcuffs on telly.'

After that, she just sat on the sofa and cried.

'Come on, Kaz,' I said. 'I'll get the ice cream. That'll make you feel better.'

She tried to smile. 'Thanks, Max.'

While Kaz was locking up, I put some ice cream in a

bowl for her. But I decided to eat mine out of the tub to save the washing up. We took it up to Kaz's room and had a sort of midnight feast – except it was only half past ten.

'I was going to ring Jason tonight,' she said. 'Only I didn't. I was too busy doing my face pack.'

'Ring him now if you want,' I said, trying to be kind in a brotherly sort of way. 'I don't suppose he'll be in bed yet. He probably spends ages in the bathroom putting stuff on his spots.'

Kaz started howling again and flung herself face down on the bed.

'What?' I said. 'I'm being nice, aren't I? What's the matter?'

'Jason will never want to speak to me if he thinks I belong to a family of criminals.'

I give up! My sister makes a drama out of everything.

Anyway, by the time I'd finished off the ice cream (Kaz wasn't hungry so I had to eat hers) she was beginning to calm down.

'We'd better get ready for bed, I suppose,' she said. 'You know we promised Dad.'

'OK. I can't wait till Dad gets back and tells us what it's like in a real prison. I bet there are cockroaches and things.'

'Max!'

'And I bet it smells.'

I thought it was brilliant being in the house on our own. It was like an adventure. You know – Dad gets captured. Kids have to fend for themselves – or starve.

After what had happened, I was bursting with great ideas. So I went back to my room to write the next chapter of my best-selling novel.

# CHAPTER 4

Watt was in a quandary. This was difficult as he wasn't sure what a quandary was. He needed money and, although he had the Jewels of Jaybal, he couldn't sell them yet – not while the Black Serpents were looking for him. They were a fiendish lot and his magic was no protection against theirs. No. The only thing to do was to lie low for a while.

One night, as he was lying low on his mattress made of old straw, there was a terrible banging at the door. Watt looked out of the window. A battalion of the Black Serpents – there must have been a hundred – were pounding their fists against the front door. But worse than the deafening noise was the stink of their putrid breath as it drifted into the cottage. Watt's stomach turned over and immediately went on strike.

'The Black Serpents have come for me,' Watt said with his hand clapped over his mouth. 'Well, I'm not scared. I'm ready to face them. Let them try and take me.'

Foolishly, he flung open the door and the Black Serpents rushed in like a tidal wave, knocking Watt to the ground.

'Help!' he yelled as their sweaty feet pounded

across his face. First they went one way, into the cottage, and then they went the other as they came out, which was very hard on Watt's face. Not until the last foot had left its imprint, did he realise that the Black Serpents had not come looking for him. The truth was, they had come for his dad.

Watt prised himself up off the floor and rubbed the circulation back into his nose. Then he leaned out of the window. 'Stop!' he yelled. But it was no good. They were dragging Dad out of the house like a helpless rag doll.

Watt couldn't stand by and do nothing.

'I'll follow them to the ends of the earth, if necessary,' he said to himself. 'Whatever happens, I'll rescue Dad and bring him home.'

He ran over to the cupboard where he kept his superhero cloak and helmet. He pulled the helmet on his head but when he reached in the cupboard to get the cloak, he found it had disappeared.

This chapter had taken me a whole fifteen minutes to write and I was whacked! I had just turned off the light when I heard a knocking at the door. Not more police, surely? I went to Kaz's room where I found her curled up with a pillow over her face. So I prodded her.

She flung the pillow away. 'Stop it! Just go away, Max! Leave me alone! Aren't things bad enough?'

'There's someone at the door,' I said.

That shut her up.

She turned and listened. There was another knock.

'Dad said not to answer if anybody came,' she said.

'OK then. We won't,' I said and went back to my bedroom.

I pulled the curtains back and looked out. There was a long, black, flashy car parked in the road and two men were at the door. Probably mates of Dad. Probably calling on the way home from the pub. But then . . . maybe not. What mate of Dad's has a car like that? I thought.

I waited for them to go away but they didn't. The next thing I heard was a key in the lock – or some kind of metal tool. Whatever it was, the two men were messing about with our front door. Were they burglars? Should I rush down and beat them up? Should I call for the SWAT team for back-up. I couldn't decide. Then there was the noise of splintering wood. Unbelievable! They were forcing the door open!

But why? It wasn't as if we had a decent telly they could steal.

Footsteps down the hall and one of the men called. 'Hey! Mark Westall.'

Silence.

'You hidin' or somethink?'

Pause.

'Mr Holland sent us. You're in deep trouble you are. So you'd better show yourself.'

This was getting really scary. What should I do now?

# Chapter 5

Dad is arrested for a diamond robbery. Then thugs break into our house...I'd watched too many detective films not to make a connection.

I dashed across the landing to Kaz's room. I thought she'd be scared. Girls scare easily in my experience.

When I opened her door, she was sitting on the bed. Of course, she pretended she wasn't frightened – but I knew different.

'What's going on, Max? Who's downstairs?'

'Dunno. But I think they're something to do with the Hatton Garden Case,' I said darkly.

Of course she didn't believe me. I'm only her kid brother.

We sat on the edge of the bed listening to the sounds in the living room. BANG! CRASH! They started turning furniture over, emptying cupboards. BOOM! SMASH! They were making a real mess by the sound of things.

'Thugs!' Kaz wailed.

'Told you!'

Then the noises stopped.

'They're talking,' Kaz said, 'but I can't hear what they're saying. Can you?'

I couldn't. It had been ages since my ears had had a serious clean-out. Still I stayed cool and thought about what a superhero would do in a situation like this. (I had a wide knowledge of superheroes – Batman, Superman, the lot, because of my in-depth reading of comics.) In seconds, I came up with the solution. I flung myself on the floor, wriggled out onto the landing, commando style, right to the top of the stairs. I lay there with my hands pushing my ears forwards so that I could catch every word.

'What we gonna do, Tone?' said one, in a stupid, droning voice.

'Dunno, Mickey,' said Tone. 'Can't see no bag down here.'

'No. No bag.'

'No.'

'We gotta find it, Tone.'

'Yeah, I know. Mr H said so.'

'Yeah. The bag's got the stuff in it.'

'We could look upstairs, yeah?'

'Yeah.'

'Right.'

'Right.'

I realised that, as soon as they walked into the hall, they'd see me – so I scrambled to my feet. Ooops! I didn't make it. I fell down again. The lace of my left trainer got caught under my right foot. I went flat on my face with a loud thud and immediately, the thugs appeared at the bottom of the stairs. Tone and Mickey. Like a comic double act. One tall, skinny and hairy. One short, bald and fat. What a pair!

When they saw me, they came thundering up the stairs, the short, fat, bald one first, puffing and panting. The skinny one behind.

'Kaz, run for it!' I yelled.

Then Baldy yelled, 'Oy! Whatchoo doin'?' and tried to grab me. No way! I jumped up and shoved him hard with my right foot. He wobbled and teetered, trying to keep his balance, but he couldn't. In the end, he fell backwards down the stairs, screaming, 'Aaaaaaaaaagh!' and landed on top of the skinny one. There they lay in a great heap, their arms and legs flailing about as they tried to get up.

What a laugh! But I couldn't stand watching them – it was time for action.

'Come on!' I shouted. 'We've got to get out of here.'

'How?'

I pointed to the landing window. 'Through there.'

While she was fiddling with the catch, I ran into Dad's room. Why? Because I knew what the men were looking for. They were looking for the bag I'd found in Dad's car. Dean Holland must have left it behind in the mad dash to catch his plane. Probably stuffed full of diamonds.

Whatever... those thugs weren't going to get it.

By the time Tone and Mickey had reached the top of the stairs, Kaz was through the window and onto the roof of the kitchen. I was following her with the bag tucked under my arm.

It was dark out there but T&M wouldn't come after us. They'd stay behind and search for the bag. (They didn't know I'd got it. Tee hee!) I guessed they'd spend ages searching through the bedrooms for it. When they couldn't find it . . . well . . . then they'd probably come looking for us.

'They might tie us up and torture us,' I said. 'I've seen that happen in films.'

Kaz snorted and said I was being stupid. She thought we should go and hide somewhere.

'We'll go to the shed,' she said as she slid down the drainpipe.

It was a hopeless suggestion. 'That would be the first place they'd look,' I said.

'Then where?'

'Dad's lockup. They won't know where it is and we can sleep in the car and go home in the morning. Dad should be back by then.'

I think she was quite impressed even though she didn't say so.

Dad's lockup wasn't far, but to get there we first had to get out of our back garden. Not easy! Then we'd have to cross three other gardens and climb several fences before we reached the road. James Bond could do it – but could we?

Garden 1: The security lights suddenly flashed on and we were trapped in the beam just like in one of those prison escape films. We tore across the grass as fast as we could and flung ourselves over the fence into . . .

Garden 2: where a dog came out of its kennel. Black and vicious. It bared its teeth and then it started barking like mad. Kaz was dead scared. Luckily it was on a chain so we kept near the fence and climbed straight into . . .

Garden 3: where a crowd of people were in the house, having a party or something. If one of them looked out of the window, we'd be spotted.

It would have helped if Kaz had been better at climbing fences.

'I'm stuck,' she squealed at the last fence.

I had to help her over of course and then she caught her jeans. 'Oh no! My best ones. They're ripped!'

She wailed and moaned. Moan, moan, moan.

'They're ruined and I've nothing to wear tomorrow night.'

I ask you, is a pair of jeans that important? There we were in the middle of the night being chased (well, maybe) by dangerous criminals and all she could do was go on about her jeans. This wouldn't happen to James Bond.

Once we were out into Waterloo Road, we hadn't far to go.

'Keep your eyes peeled for police cars,' I said. 'They might wonder why two kids are out late at night.'

Luckily, I saw one just in time. I dived into a shop doorway and pulled Kaz after me, clamping my hand over her mouth in case she screamed. I stayed there, with my back pressed up against the wall. I could feel her struggling. She was probably terrified.

Once the police car had passed, I let her go. Did she thank me for being so quick off the mark? No!

'Why did you do that?' she yelled and pushed me away in a very ungrateful manner. 'You're crazy, you are!'

I ignored my hysterical sister and went ahead towards Dingley Street. It was starting to rain – so I decided to run and get to the lockups as fast as possible. Kaz followed on behind.

There were ten lockups round the back of Dingley Street. Dad's was the end one.

'This place is such a dump,' Kaz whinged when we got there. 'Why doesn't Dad find somewhere better? All my friends have proper garages. This is embarrassing.'

I said something witty in reply but she didn't notice. She was more concerned with getting inside and out of the rain. It wasn't that easy. There was a chain and padlock on the door of Dad's lockup.

'We can't get in,' she moaned. 'Now my hair's going to be ruined. Honestly! Everything is going from bad to worse!'

For me this was just another problem to be solved. Another twist in the adventure of two kids struggling to escape dangers in a criminal world. I'd seen a film last week where the hero had to climb on the roof and enter a building through a skylight. He had to smash the glass and everything. Of course, I could have done that – but I didn't have to. I knew where Dad kept the key. It was in the top of the drainpipe, so I just shinned up and fetched it out.

'Am I brilliant? Or am I perfect?' I said, dangling the key in front of Kaz. Then I unlocked the door and opened it.

Not that Kaz appreciated my genius. She just gave me one of her looks and pushed past me.

Luckily, Dad hadn't locked his car. Probably forgot. He's been in a real state since that phonecall he'd had from Dean Holland. It must have wound him up. Made him real twitchy.

'I'll take the back seat,' Kaz said, climbing into the car. 'I need more room than you.'

It didn't bother me.

'This is cool,' I said. 'I've never slept in a car. I've not even been camping without a grown-up. And this is loads better than camping in a tent, eh, Kaz?'

Kaz grunted.

'I can't wait to tell Jamie,' I said. 'He's never slept in a car either. He'll be dead jealous.'

'Shh!'

'He's never had his dad dragged off to prison, either. In fact, nobody in our class has had their dad taken by the Bill. I'm the first.'

'SHH!'

'Jamie's never had dangerous thugs smash up his house and come chasing after him…'

'MAX! WILL YOU SHUT IT?' Kaz said. 'This isn't an adventure in one of your stupid comics. Go to sleep and let's hope everything will be back to normal tomorrow.'

But I didn't go to sleep. I found a torch and a notebook in the glove compartment and I wrote chapter 5 of my novel.

# CHAPTER 5

As soon as Watt saw the empty cupboard, he guessed where the cloak was. His kid sister, Starlight, had taken it to play with. She was always doing that. She loved dressing up. (Did I mention that he had a kid sister? Watt's dad had found her abandoned in the wood, one night on his way home from work. Even though it was a cloudy, cold and miserable night, he called her Starlight. But she was just an ordinary human baby, not brilliantly intelligent like Watt.)

Watt went into her room to look for the Magic Cloak. Starlight was asleep so he leaned over and shook her gently.

'Quick,' he said. 'I have to find my cloak. Where is it?'

She rubbed her eyes the way little kids do and smiled up at her brother. 'Hewo, Watt. I got your cwoak,' she said, pulling it from under her pillow. 'You're not cwoth with me for bowowing it, are you?'

Most boys would have gone ballistic – or ground their teeth at the very least – but not Watt. He had perfect control over his temper and didn't even groan. (Which just goes to show how superhuman he was.)

'Of course I'm not cross,' he said soothingly. She was only six after all.

He took the cloak, flung it over his shoulder and raced outside. But by then, the Black Serpents were nowhere to be seen – and neither was Dad. Our superhero stared into the darkness, his heart sinking faster than a lead balloon.

'They've gone,' he said – which was stating the obvious. He climbed the nearest tree in order to see into the wood and beyond. There was no sign of the Black Serpents – but there was something much, much worse.

'Eeeeeeeek!' he screeched. 'It's the deadly Krill Gang. What are they doing here?'

The Krill Gang were a rough lot who liked to go down to the pub after the match, drink it dry and then run wild. Each one was as tall as two men and had the strength of ten. Every morning they used a sanding machine to polish their heads until they were so smooth that they could be seen for miles. Our hero had had an argument with them once as they staggered out of The Blacksmith and Nail in the High Street. Using wit and cunning, he had got the better of them but ever since, the Krill Gang had been determined to be revenged.

Up in the tree, Redwon, superhero, swallowed nervously. 'They probably won't recognise me dressed like this,' he said to himself. 'But I need to know what they're up to.'

He tuned in his mega-sensitive hearing, leaned out of the tree and listened. The Krill Gang spoke their own strange language of grunts and howls and silly noises. But this was not a problem as Redwon's brain could translate every sound.

As he listened to what they were saying, his blood ran cold. Up until now, they had no idea where he lived but it was clear from what he overheard, that they had found out and were planning to kill him. (It was the kind of thing they did on Saturday nights for a bit of a laugh.) Redwon realised that they were heading for the cottage where Starlight was fast asleep and they would be sure to kill her if they felt like it. He would have to move fast if he was going to save his sister.

He slid down the tree trunk (very rough, very painful) and ran back into the cottage.

'Starlight!' he yelled as he pounded up the stairs.

The little girl sat up in her bed, amazed to see a superhero in her room.

'Don't be afraid, kid,' he said soothingly. 'I'm here to help you.'

'Why?' she asked in an innocent kind of way.

'Because some nasty men are coming to kill you,' Redwon said gently.

'Oh no!' she squealed.

'Jump on my back and I'll take you to safety.'

'Thank you,' she said. 'But who are you?'

'Just call me Redwon.'

Starlight clung gratefully onto his back as he leapt out of the window and flew away just as the killer Krill Gang came into view.

# Chapter 6

Sleeping in the car was OK. I slept like a log until I was woken by the William Tell Overture. It went on and on, getting louder until I realised that Kaz had Dad's mobile in her pocket.

'Kaz!' I said. 'Kaz! The mobile's ringing.' But I had to poke her to make her wake up and answer it.

'Mmmm?' she said into the mouthpiece. She was still half asleep.

'Kaz, can you hear me? It's Dad.'

'DAD!' she yelled, suddenly wide awake.

'DAD?' I yelled and reached into the back seat to grab the phone – but Kaz turned away so that it was out of my reach.

I couldn't hear what Dad said but this is how the conversation went (Kaz told me afterwards).

**Dad:** I hope I didn't get you out of bed.

**Kaz:** No, Dad. Where are you?

**Dad:** I'm phoning from the station.

**Kaz:** The railway station?

**Dad:** The police station. I'm still under arrest.

**Kaz:** Oh no!

**Dad:** I tried the house phone but it was out of order. So I rang my mobile. I knew I'd left it on the table. I just hoped you'd hear it.

**Kaz:** I did.

**Dad:** You'd better get somebody to look at the house phone. There must be a fault.

**Kaz:** It's not that, Dad.

**Dad:** What?

**Kaz:** Two men broke in last night and wrecked the place. They must have damaged the phone.

Apparently Dad went ballistic. And when she told him about us climbing out of the window and sleeping all night in the car...BOOM! TZCHAAHHHH! BAAAHHGH! Dad exploded. Kaz held the mobile away from her face. She was in danger of permanent damage to her hearing.

After he'd calmed down, he said that we mustn't go back home. Not yet. Not until things were sorted. He wanted us to stay with Grandad in Tooting. Personally, I thought this was a bad idea. How can you compare sleeping at Grandad's with spending the night in a lockup?

**Kaz:** I nearly forgot. We've got the bag they were looking for, Dad.

**Dad:** What bag?

**Kaz:** The one Max found in your car. Shall we take it to the police?

**Dad:** In my car?

**Kaz:** Yes.

**Dad:** The car...(Kaz said he seemed to be thinking about something and he didn't speak for ages.)

**Kaz:** Yes, Max found it when he cleaned your car.

**Dad:** Found it? Er...NO! No, definitely don't take it to the police. Whatever you do, don't do that! Keep it safe somewhere.

**Kaz:** Why?

**Dad:** It must be Dean Holland's bag and he's the crook. Not me. I don't want the police to think I've got anything to do with it – whatever it is. Tell Grandad what's happened. He'll know what to do. I'll ring you at his house.

And that was that. Dad had to go.

After that call, it was obvious to anyone with a knowledge of detective stories, that the bag was mega important. Yet we hadn't opened it up and looked inside.

'It'll be stuffed with diamonds,' I said. 'I know it. I'm going to look.'

Kaz said I wouldn't be able to see much because it was dark in the lockup. (Dad hadn't got around to fixing the light.) She said I should wait until we were at Grandad's house. But I couldn't.

I unzipped the bag and plunged my hand inside. I could feel something soft. Probably clothes. I swished my fingers around underneath and felt something hard. Which turned out to be a pair of trainers.

'I can't feel anything else,' I said. 'Who would want to steal clothes and a pair of trainers?'

'Dummy,' said Kaz. 'They're just a cover-up. If there are any diamonds, they'll be hidden in a secret compart-

50

ment. Stop messing, Max. Let's get moving. I'll feel safer at Grandad's house.'

We set off down Streatham High Street to catch the bus. I was feeling faint with hunger. I hadn't eaten a thing since the sausage, bacon, beans and chips I'd had the night before. No wonder walking was an effort. Kaz had some money in her pocket and I persuaded her to buy two packets of crisps, which I managed to finish off before the bus arrived. (Kaz was on a diet. That's why I had to eat hers as well.)

The bus ride was seriously boring so I won't tell you about that. It took ages and ages but when we got to Tooting, the bus stopped right outside Sainsbury's – which was lucky. We could pick up something for breakfast. OK. So I'd had crisps but they were emergency rations only.

'We've no money left,' said Kaz. 'Don't make a fuss! You can have breakfast at Grandad's.'

Sisters don't understand that boys' energy levels soon drop to danger point. By then, I could only drag my feet slowly over the pavement and soon I was several metres behind her. She didn't even look round!

Grandad lived at 101 Condonkin Road (or Donkey Road as he called it). It was a long road with houses on either side. Old houses with little front gardens concreted over for parking cars.

Not Grandad's though. His front garden was filled with gnomes and frogs and old chimney pots. It was great.

'Hurry up, Max,' called Kaz, not caring about my

poor physical condition. 'We're here now.' She pushed
open the small wooden gate and, by the time I'd caught
up, she was banging the knocker.

'This is going to be a surprise for him,' she said.

But Grandad didn't come to the door.

'You have to knock louder, Kaz. I'll do it. He could be
in the back.'

So I gave it loads of welly.

No answer.

'I don't like it,' I said. 'Supposing he's in there, tied
up by the Mob.'

'What mob?' said Kaz. 'He's probably gone shopping.
We'll have to wait.'

Wait? Not me. I knew where Grandad kept the key. It
was in the oldest gnome. The one with the chipped nose,
the peeling paint and the broken fishing rod. It wasn't
the kind of thing sisters would know.

I put the key in the lock, eager to get inside for
something to eat, when Mrs MacDonald next door
parted her net curtains and waved at us. In seconds she
was out of the front door.

'Och, it's lovely to see you,' she said. 'I thought it
wouldn't be long before you arrived. I thought they'd
ring you.'

I glanced at Kaz and shrugged.

'I expect it was a real shock, wasn't it? Aye it was a
shock for me sure enough. Terrible. Terrible.'

Kaz nudged me and I nodded like a robot and said,
'Yes, terrible.'

Mrs MacDonald was always a bit nutty so I didn't worry that I hadn't a clue what she was talking about.

'But where's your dad?' she said.

'He's coming later,' said Kaz, quick as a flash. 'He had to work today.'

'Then I expect you'll be going to the hospital on your own,' she said. 'Or I'll come with you, if you like.'

I looked at Kaz and Kaz looked at me. Hospital? What was going on?

'I've told him a thousand times – "Finbar," I said, "one of these days you'll catch your foot on that ruined old stair carpet and you'll fall and break your neck. Mark my words!" But would he listen? Oh, no!'

'So he broke his neck?' I suggested.

'No. His leg,' she said. 'I was the one who sent for the ambulance, you know.' She puffed out her chest, crossed her arms and looked pleased with herself.

'That was very good of you,' said Kaz. 'We're going to stay here for a few days so we'll make sure Grandad has everything he needs.' (Which I thought was a brilliant thing to say. Well done, Sis!)

Eventually, we said goodbye and walked into the house.

No sooner had the door shut behind us than I had a terrible thought.

'Oh no!' I said and clapped my hand on my forehead.

'Don't worry about Grandad, Max. He'll be OK.'

'I wasn't,' I said. 'It's worse than that.'

'What?'

53

'I've missed football practice. It went clean out of my head.'

Kaz looked totally disgusted. But then she didn't realise that today was crucial. Today was the preparation for the final game – the one which was make or break for the Cup. We were in with a real chance this year. We'd even got our own football chant:

**Park Street School, Park Street School,**
**Here we go again.**
**Park Street School, Park Street School,**
**With our team of men,**
**Feared by the bad,**
**Cheered by the good,**
**Park Street School, Park Street School, Park**
**Street School.**

HOW COULD I FORGET THE VITAL PRACTICE? I looked at my watch. In ten minutes, Jamie would be leaving and expecting to see me on the field. I'd got to talk to him. Let him know what had happened so he can tell Old Bagsy, our sports teacher.

I ran into the living room, picked up the phone and dialled Jamie's number. It rang for such a long time, I thought he'd already left.

'Hello?'

It was Craig.

'It's Max,' I panted. 'Can I speak to Jamie? It's urgent.'

There was a pause and I could hear my heart beating while I waited.

'Sorry, Max. You've just missed him. Can I give him a message or something. Is anything wrong?'

I couldn't tell him about Dad, could I? He said not to tell anyone.

'Grandad's had an accident,' I said, 'and we're staying at his house for a few days. We came over this morning. That's why I've missed the practice.'

In a way, it was the truth so I didn't feel too bad.

'Sorry about your grandad,' said Craig. 'Does he live near?'

'Not really.'

'Is there any way I can help?'

'Thanks,' I said. 'But we're OK. Just tell Jamie I phoned.'

I was feeling mega depressed after the phone call. So I pulled the exercise book out of my pocket and wrote chapter 6.

# CHAPTER 6

As Redwon flew over the wood with Starlight on his back, the Krill gangleader, Omph, looked up and spotted him.

'Blerrrr thrumpt ahhhgh!' he shouted and pointed skywards. 'Zooool!'

This latter noise was the war cry of the Krill Gang and meant certain death. Was Redwon afraid? No way!

'Zooool to you,' the superhero yelled back and he kept flying. Even when clouds gathered over him and fierce winds blew and torrential rain began to pour, even then he carried on. Until he spotted a small, grassy island just like the one he had seen last week in a holiday brochure (off the coast of Greece, £700 for 14 nights, breakfast included).

He dipped towards it and soon landed – though with a bit of a bump as Redwon was in the early stages of his flying career. Any pilot will tell you that landing is the toughest challenge.

'I'll light a fire and you'll be warm,' said Redwon to his sister. 'You need to get those clothes dry.'

'You're so bwave and clever,' said Starlight, who was wearing her favourite pink satin teddy bear pyjamas and hated to think that they might be ruined.

Redwon quickly chopped down a tree and made a roaring fire on which he cooked sausages and beans. He was pleased to have escaped the Krill Gang but now he must find out where the Black Serpents had taken Dad.

'I've been thinking,' he said. 'Once your pyjamas are dry, we must go and find Grandol, the Wise One of Tatam.'

'Who is he?' asked Starlight.

'He is a very brainy old man who knows practically everything,' said Redwon.

'But you know evwyfing, Thuperhewo.'

Redwon smiled and patted her on the head. 'I don't know where your father is,' he said. 'We need Grandol to tell us how to find him.'

# Chapter 7

'We're going to the hospital,' said Kaz before I'd finished the seriously cheesy sandwich I'd made.

'You go,' I said. 'I've got training to do.'

I'd already missed today's practice and I could lose muscle tone if I didn't work out. I had to keep myself in peak condition.

'If you think you're going to spend the afternoon messing around with a football in Grandad's garden ...'

Messing around! Huh! This was one of the most important things in my life and she made it sound pathetic! Girls!

'You're coming to see Grandad. If I can give up a date with Jason, you can go without football for a day.'

How could she compare football with Jazzo-boy! And what difference would a couple of hours make? Grandad wouldn't mind waiting. He was dead keen on football himself. He used to play for a team back in Ireland. He's still pretty good even at his age – well, he was before he broke his leg.

But Kaz insisted. I had to go to the hospital. Typical.

Just before we left, the phone went. I picked it up, hoping it might be Dad but it was a mate of Grandad's, called Dave. I think they went to the pub together. Dave hadn't heard about the accident so I filled him in. He was shocked, of course.

'Pity,' he said. 'He's missed a dead cert in the 3.30. Bluebell Flier. Great horse. He'd have made his fortune. You tell him that when you go to see him.'

Kaz tutted when I repeated the conversation. 'Huh!' she said. 'Wasting his pension betting on horses. How stupid is that?'

She thinks Grandad's interest in racing isn't cool but I don't see what's wrong with it. He's interested in loads of things. It's better than watching the telly all day – although he does watch quite a bit in the afternoon 'cos that's when they show the horse racing.

We'd gone out to the hall and the phone went again.

'I'm not answering it,' Kaz said. 'It'll only be another of Grandad's drinking cronies. Let's go.'

Personally, I can't stand to hear a phone ring and not answer it. So I went and lifted the receiver. This time, it was the hospital. They wanted to know some stuff about Grandad – full name, address, next of kin. So I passed the phone to Kaz. I don't do information.

When she'd finished, we finally left. I made up for my lack of football practice by finding an abandoned drinks can which I dribbled all the way down Condonkin Road. Kaz pretended she wasn't with me. Who cares?

The hospital was massive and we had to go up in the lift to get to the ward where Grandad was. We knew we'd found the right one because we could hear Grandad's voice while we were still out in the corridor.

'Nurse! Nurse!' he was calling. 'Will you be bringing

me a cup of tea, my lovely? My throat's that parched it feels like a parrot cage.'

When we turned the corner, we could see him at the end of the ward, lying on a bed with his left leg in plaster, waving his arms, trying to attract the attention of a passing nurse.

'Grandad,' I yelled and ran towards him. I only narrowly avoided a doctor in a white coat who stepped into my path. I didn't trip. But he threw his notes all over the floor and made a real mess.

'Max!' called Grandad. 'Good to see you, lad. I knew someone would let you know I was here.'

'That's an excellent plaster,' I said. 'There's enough room for the whole team to sign when you come over to watch us play.'

'Do you think so, son?' he grinned. 'Well, that's all right then.'

Before we went to the hospital, Kaz decided not to tell Grandad about Dad until the time was right. She said that she didn't want to shock him because he was a fragile old man and might have a heart attack or something. So I told him about Dave instead.

'Dave, you say? A message, eh? What was it?'

'Something about a dead cert called Bluebell Flier.'

'Say again, son. Word for word. What exactly did he say?'

'He said, "Tell him he's missed a dead cert in the 3.30. Bluebell Flier. He'd have made his fortune." That's was all.'

Grandad's eyes grew wide and he suddenly looked panicky.

'That's all, you say. Aye. But it's not all. It's a tragedy. Dave doesn't often call things a dead cert. Not Dave. If he says a horse is a winner then I mustn't miss it.' He looked down at his watch. 'Get me down to the bookie's quick and we'll make it before they're off. Find a wheelchair, son. There's one in the corridor.'

Kaz went into a tizzy. 'Grandad! We can't take you out of the hospital. You're ill.'

He winked at her. 'I'm not in the least bit ill, sweetheart. It's only the leg. Sure, a little trip down the High Street will do me a world of good. All that fresh air. And who will miss me for an hour or so, eh?'

I got a wheelchair, covered Grandad with a blanket and started pushing him down the ward.

'Mr O'Malley!'

The words stopped us in our tracks. I wheeled the chair round and faced a large nurse in a blue uniform.

'Where are you going?' she said, walking towards us. She narrowed her eyes, pressed her lips together and looked mean. Very mean. It wasn't going to be easy to get past her.

But I was wrong. This nurse was no match for my grandad. He looked straight at her and gave her one of his beaming smiles. Mum used to say he could charm the birds off the trees. And he could, too.

'Sure, my grandchildren are just taking me for a wee smoke and a cup of tea,' he said. 'It's a terrible thing when you're addicted to the weed at my age. I've tried to give it up, but I'm just a weak old man.' The nurse tutted and frowned a bit. 'And a nice cup of tea would be a great pleasure, sure it would,' he went on. Then he raised his eyebrows. 'Will that be all right, nurse?'

'Well . . . ' she hesitated. 'Back in half an hour. You've had a shock and you need your rest, you know.'

Grandad nodded. 'I'll be back before you know I'm gone,' he said. 'You nurses are angels, sure you are. Angels.'

She blushed and her mouth twitched into a little smile. 'Oh, go on!' she said.

So we did.

Under directions from Grandad, I pushed the wheelchair at top speed down the High Street, clearing a path right through the shoppers. Zoom! Our only problem was one inconsiderate shopkeeper who left vases of flowers on the pavement outside his shop and some of them spilled. There were flowers and water everywhere but I managed to push them aside OK so Grandad didn't get wet.

He just kept shouting, 'Come on, Max! Faster, lad! Faster!'

We had about a hundred metres to go when I noticed the police. There were two of them walking towards us, side by side – obviously on the lookout for shifty characters. It suddenly struck me that they'd be carrying 'Wanted' lists in their pockets – photographs even – and I might be on it. When they got closer, would they recognise me as the Town Park Flower Thief and arrest me on the spot? Or would they think I was just an ordinary kid? It wasn't something I could risk.

I decided to disappear off the High Street – fast, like a rat down a hole. If I ran, I could make it to the bookie's shop before they spotted me. I'd be safe in there.

'You push the wheelchair,' I said to Kaz. 'I'll run ahead and tell the bookie Grandad's on his way.'

Kaz yelled after me – something about me being too young to go inside a betting shop. I didn't hear properly.

My sprinting speed is pretty good, what with all the training, and I was soon at the bookie's. Then I did a brilliant swerve, a lunge at the handle and pushed the door open. I didn't know someone was coming out. Anyway, I helped him get up.

'What's going on?' called a man from behind a counter. 'Coppers after you?'

I stopped in my tracks. Was it a joke? Or did he have inside knowledge? Then he burst out laughing – but I wondered if he knew who I really was. I was even more suspicious when he said, 'You shouldn't be in here. No kids. It's illegal.'

Anyway, I kept my cool. 'Mind if I sit here and write my novel while I wait for my grandad?' I said. 'He's on his way. He won't be long.'

I think he was dead impressed to have a novelist in his shop. I don't suppose he got many of those.

63

# CHAPTER 7

Grandol, the Wise One of Tatam, lived in a high turret built on a cliff on the far side of the island. Redwon knew this because there had been an article about him in the local paper. Not only was he wise – telling people what to do and that – but he was amazing at predicting winners at the local races. People swore by him.

Redwon and Starlight set off to find him and managed to get there in time for tea.

'Greetings, Wise One,' said Redwon as they landed on the ledge outside his very desirable detached four-bedroom turret. 'We need help to track down a man who has been taken by the Black Serpents.'

'Pleath help uth,' pleaded Starlight. 'He'th my daddy,'

The Wise One smiled wisely, as he picked bits of yesterday's dinner out of his beard. 'I will help you my child,' he said. 'Let us go down to the beach and I will draw you a map in the sand.'

Redwon couldn't think why he didn't use paper. But Grandol was known to have some funny ways.

Once down on the shore, the Wise One took out a long stick and began to mark out the route in the sand.

'The way is long,' said Grandol. 'But you are brave, Redwon. Keep going this way and you will surely save her father.'

He was about to draw the final part when he suddenly clasped his hand to his chest and cried out. 'Aaaaaaaaaaagh!'

'What's wrong?' cried Redwon.

But the old man couldn't answer. His face turned to chalk, his legs turned to jelly and he collapsed on the sand on top of the map, which ruined it completely.

'Quick!' cried the superhero. 'There is no time to lose. We must take him to the White Witch of Warwick. She will soon cure him and he can draw us another map.'

The White Witch lived nearby in an abandoned beer barrel (complete with an early form of central heating). She had a good reputation locally for healing the sick but, when Redwon caught up with her hanging out some washing on a blackthorn bush, he was disappointed. The washing wasn't even clean. This woman in her tatty apron and huge hobnailed boots was unlikely to bring anyone – and certainly not Grandol – back to health.

Redwon laid him in front of the beer barrel while the witch finished pegging out a pair of knickers obviously made from a worn-out pair of curtains.

At last she came across, leaned over Grandol and said, 'He's old. I can see that.' She sniffed and wiped her snotty nose with the back of her hand. 'And from the colour of his beard, he smokes like a trooper. You can't expect miracles, son.'

'You must save him!' Redwon insisted. 'He's our only hope to find Starlight's father.'

'Aaargh,' she grunted. 'There's only one thing that'll save him. I'd need the juice of the throgmirtle plant to do any good. Without that, he's a goner – and I haven't seen the throgmirtle for donkey's years.'

Redwon sighed. 'It's hopeless,' he said. 'Now Grandol will never be able to help us.'

Just as I'd finished, the door of the betting shop burst open. Grandad had arrived.

'Hold the horses!' he shouted as Kaz pushed him inside. 'Am I in time for the 3.30, Mac?'

'Ah it's you, Finbar!' the bookie called. 'Steady on! You've another five minutes, mate. I'll take your bet and then you can tell me what you're doing in pyjamas with a plaster cast on your leg. Have you been partying again?'

Grandad laughed. 'I'll tell you later, Mac. It's a long story.'

He pulled his wallet out of his pyjama jacket and

placed his bet. He was just settling down to watch the race on the TV screen, when the police walked in. Doom! So they'd finally got me. Now I'd have to own up to the Town Park Flower Robbery. Who knows – Dad and me could soon be sharing the same cell.

# Chapter 8

The police didn't arrest me. They didn't realise who I was. They probably thought I was a famous novelist writing up some notes. Observing human behaviour. Researching my book. Anyway, they gave Grandad a telling off for taking me into a betting shop and he just smiled the way he does and said, 'Ah sure, I won't let it happen again, officer.'

The policeman asked Kaz how old she was. 'You are over 18, aren't you, miss?' he said.

She blushed and nodded. It was a lie, of course. She was only sixteen – but Kaz likes people to think she looks really grown up. Especially boys.

The policewoman took me outside and we waited while Grandad collected his winnings.

'How come your grandad's still got his pyjamas on?' she asked. 'Does he always go down the High Street like that?'

I thought it was a bit of a rude comment actually. 'No,' I said. 'He's dangerously ill and should be at the hospital in bed.'

She raised her eyebrows. 'You mean he escaped?'

'Sort of.'

She pushed open the door of the betting shop and poked her head round the corner.

'Constable,' she called. 'I think you'd better hear this.'

I wish I'd kept my mouth shut. I wish I'd mentioned the hospital. They couldn't wait to m. down the High Street and even insisted on pushing the wheelchair. It was really embarrassing. They kept asking Grandad if he was all right. Of course he was. It was only a broken leg.

Anyway they took us all the way back to the ward where the boss nurse (who was seriously scary) told us all off.

Not that Grandad was bothered. When she'd gone, he just laughed. 'It was worth it, wasn't it?' he said from his bed. 'Sure, I won a tidy sum, didn't I?'

Kaz tut-tutted again and said that gambling was bad – until Grandad gave her some money to buy a new pair of jeans. That changed her mind.

He gave me some, too, which meant I'd got enough for the new football gear, at last. Brilliant!

'And this,' he said, peeling off another note, 'is for food. You'll need something for tea. Or are you going right back to Streatham tonight?'

I looked at Kaz. I knew what she was thinking. This was probably the right time to tell Grandad the truth about Dad. So we did.

It was lucky that Grandad was in bed because he went quite pale. He didn't faint or anything but he didn't speak for ages. (This is almost unheard of. Our grandad could talk for Britain.) Kaz asked me to get a cup of tea out of the machine and by the time I'd got back, he was looking better.

'Sure, there's been a mistake, my lovelies,' he said. 'Your da's a good man. He wouldn't steal diamonds, for goodness sake. I can't imagine him doing anything bad, can you?'

We agreed. We couldn't imagine Dad going in for that kind of thing.

'You mark my words, he'll be back before you know it. But...' he paused as he sipped his tea, '...what do we do about that bag, eh? And those men... They sound like a nasty pieces of work to me.'

'I've known plenty of criminals in films and stuff, Grandad,' I said. 'I'm quite used to 'em.'

We sat on the edge of the bed and went into thinking mode. Grandad was tucked up in blue blankets, frowning into the far distance. You could almost hear his brain ticking.

When he spoke at last, he said, 'There's only one thing for it. Go to the police and give them the bag. Tell them exactly what you told me. Then you go back to my house and stay there until everything's sorted and your da's back. Sure, you're old enough and sensible enough to do that, aren't you?'

I didn't think this was much of a solution but Kaz didn't comment. Instead, she put her arms round Grandad and gave him one of her rib-breaking hugs.

'Don't worry, Grandad,' she said. 'We'll get things sorted and we'll be back in the morning. OK?'

Grandad grinned. 'Nothing nicer, sweetheart,' he said. 'See you tomorrow.'

70

He settled down with the sporting page of the paper and we left the hospital.

I was seriously worried. We couldn't go to the police for two reasons. Number 1 – we'd promised Dad not to. Number 2 – if we went to the police station, I might just bump into a top rate detective and risk being recognised as the Streatham Flower Thief.

'Kaz,' I said as soon as we were outside. 'We can't go to the police station.'

She sighed in that annoying, big-sister way she has. 'Stop panicking, Max. We're not going anywhere near one. Dad gave us strict instructions. I just don't think Grandad ought to know that, do you? He'll only worry.'

Girls can be very devious.

We went up the High Street. Me to Sainsbury's. Kaz to buy a pair a jeans for her date with Jason. I definitely got the best of the deal. I don't do clothes shopping.

In the supermarket, I planned a fantastic, lip-smacking meal for Kaz. It would be miles better than her usual salad and organic yoghurt. I wanted to show her how lucky she was to have a considerate kid brother like me.

This was the menu:

Farmer Ben's Big Beef Sausages, baked beans, bubble and squeak (frozen), bacon and chips (frozen – oven kind).

Followed by:

Chocolate gateau and mint chip ice cream. Also a box of chocolates as a present for my sister (unless she wanted to share them, of course).

When I'd paid at the checkout, I crossed the High

Street to the shop where Kaz was buying her jeans. It was really girlie. Full of pink and glitter and earrings. I decided to wait outside. I wouldn't be seen dead in a place like that.

I stood there, yawning and feeling bored, when I noticed a car – long and black with big chrome bumpers – was stuck in the traffic jam in the High Street. It wasn't any old car. It was definitely the one outside our house last night. And the driver was definitely Tone (or was it Mickey?). Did it matter? The Case of the Diamond Robbery was hotting up. They must be onto us!

I ran into the shop.

'My sister,' I yelled at a scarlet-haired woman who was sitting by the till, reading a magazine. 'Where is she?'

'Cubicle,' she said and nodded towards the corner. I ran across and dragged back the curtain.

Kaz screamed and tried to cover herself.

'I'm trying things on, Max,' she wailed.

I could see that. She was white and covered in goose bumps. It was horrible!

'Go away!' she said and tried to wrap the curtain round her.

'Listen, Kaz! I've just seen a car with the thugs in it. They must have tracked us down.'

That changed her mind. She pulled on her own jeans pretty quick, threw an identical pair to the assistant and said, 'I'll take these, please.'

We left the shop and ran up the High Street. Just to make sure we weren't being followed, I used an old trick

72

I'd seen in loads of films. We took the long way back to Grandad's. Up one-way streets. Down side streets. There was no chance they could have followed us.

'Why would they...come to...Tooting looking... for us?' said Kaz who was very unfit and could do with a workout. 'It's probably...just coincidence. You haven't...told anyone where we are...have you, Max?'

'Nobody,' I said. 'Only Grandad and Mrs MacDonald, next door – and Grandad's mate, Dave.'

By the time we reached the house, Kaz was on the verge of collapse. Me? No problem. All that training was paying off.

The Case of the Diamond Robbery was seriously big league. I could feel it. Today was like the best bit in the detective film where the thugs close in on the hero. In our case it was two kids alone – Dad in gaol and Grandad in hospital. What was going to happen next?

Once inside Grandad's house, I handed Kaz the bags from Sainsbury's.

'Here's the stuff I bought,' I said and hoped she'd do the cooking. I had important work to do. If I was going to be a successful novelist, I had to keep at it. So I sat down with a bag of crisps (did I mention I'd bought a bumper pack?) and started to write chapter 8.

# CHAPTER 8

The route Grandol had begun to draw in the sand pointed westward. At least they could head in the right direction. So they set off, flying over mountains and through valleys as he had told them.

They had been flying for some time when Starlight pointed to a hillside miles below. 'What'th that, Thuperhewo?' she asked. 'There are loths of ants wunning over the gwass. Thome of them are hiding in that little box.'

Redwon glanced down. Just as well! Those ants were no ants! They were armies of Black Serpents swarming over the countryside. And that box was no box. It was a huge concrete office block.

'Well spotted, Starlight,' he said. 'I think we've found the headquarters of the Black Serpents. We'll break into the main building and maybe find out where they have taken your father.'

Redwon fixed his laser vision and tracked in on a suitable landing site on the headquarters building.

'Hold tight,' he yelled and zoomed towards the roof at supersonic speed. They landed with a

74

soft thud this time, as Redwon's piloting skills had miraculously improved. Starlight stayed on the roof to keep watch while Redwon leapt through a window (unfortunately closed at the time) and crept along the corridor dripping a trail of blood behind him. Then he broke into an office with several computers.

Using his computer skills, he soon managed to find details of Dad's capture in the file marked 'Kidnapping'. There was all the information he needed – along with details of the planned assassination – 'Make this a long lingering death if possible on account of his long lingering legs'.

'Brilliant!' said Redwon, stepping out into the corridor as he tucked the printout under his shirt.

Unfortunately, a guard called Three Eyes had spotted the trail of blood, followed it and bumped into Redwon in the doorway. The sight of blood made Three Eyes feel dizzy and Redwon was able to slip past him. Even so, Three Eyes managed to sound the alarm.

In minutes, legions of Black Serpents were swarming up the hill towards Redwon. This would have been the end for most heroes – but not for Redwon. He leaped out of a window (open), pulled out a Power Sword (standard issue with all Superhero Magic Cloaks) and faced them.

As the Black Serpents ran to attack him, he

swung the Power Sword at them. Swish! Swipe! One by one, they fell down dead, until only the biggest one – the leader, called Maggoo, was left.

Maggoo and Redwon fought for an hour, slithering and sliding over dead bodies (or sometimes just bits of bodies – such as severed arms and legs or bits of gut). It made fighting very difficult.

By then, even Redwon was getting tired. For a nanosecond, he let his concentration slip and in that time, he suddenly felt a sharp, agonising pain in his arm. Maggoo had cut into his flesh. Blood was gushing everywhere, dripping on the ground, making a great gooey pool and ruining his clothes.

'Don't think you've won,' Redwon shouted and quickly pulled off his trousers and wrapped them round the wound, regardless of the fact that he was wearing fluorescent pink underpants.

He lunged at his enemy, who – dazzled by the underpants – was caught off guard. The Power Sword pierced his hairy chest. He screamed and immediately fell down dead, which was a great relief.

All the fighting and bleeding made Redwon really hungry. His kind of superhero could not survive without chocolate and barbecue-flavoured crisps.

Luckily, Starlight – who had been waiting on the roof all this time – had spotted that they were near their own home town and she knew there was a small supermarket in the High Street.

'Follow me, Thuperhewo,' she said, tugging his arm. 'It won't take long.'

By the time they reached the supermarket, Redwon was wilting with hunger. Somehow, he staggered through the door and leaned for support on the till.

'You're starving,' said a kind girl with blue eyes who was working at the checkout. She was the most beautiful thing Redwon had ever seen. She was a cross between Snow White (the Disney version) and the barmaid in 'Coronation Street' – only blonde.

'Have this,' she whispered. 'I brought it for my lunch.'

'Thank you,' said Redwon, and bit into a chocolate bar with crunchy mint filling.

He felt better immediately and he leaned towards her, winked and raised the right side of his mouth. That smile was irresistible.

'You may not know it,' he whispered into her ear, 'but I am someone special and one day you will have your reward.'

The girl looked at him and suddenly realised who he was. Her eyes widened in amazement, the colour drained from her cheeks and she fainted.

# Chapter 9

Kaz hadn't even started cooking by the time I'd finished chapter 8. She'd been trying on her new jeans.

'What d'you think, Max?' she said. 'The woman in the shop said I looked really slim in them. Aren't they gorgeous?'

To be honest, they looked like every other pair of jeans she'd had – but I said, 'Mmm,' just to please her.

When she left the living room, she took the mobile to talk to lover-boy Jason.

'Don't pick up Grandad's phone, if it rings,' she called out as she went upstairs. 'We don't want anybody else knowing we're here.'

'What if Dad rings?'

'If we don't answer, he'll try the mobile. OK?'

'OK.'

I was starving but as it was obvious that Kaz wasn't going to cook, I went into the kitchen to start.

I reached into the fridge for Farmer Ben's Big Beef Sausages. But there in front of me was the ice cream. Chocolate Mint Crisp wasn't my first choice so I thought I ought to test it. Blueberry Crisp was my favourite. I'd had it at the pictures when I went to see an ace film about a spider from outer space. Sainsbury's didn't stock it. Pity. They don't know what they're missing. Still, I enjoyed the Chocolate Mint and I left some for Kaz to try later. She was on a diet so I didn't have to leave much. Now for the cooking.

I'd liked cooking ever since Dad showed me. I pretend to be one of those chefs on TV. I talk while I'm doing things. I explain cooking techniques and that. Frying the sausages and bacon. Opening the tin of beans and dropping them into a pan. Watching chips in the oven through that little glass window in the door. If you're not an experienced cook, it can be tricky doing all these things at once – but keep on trying, that's what I say.

When everything was cooked, I arranged the chips on the plate in an artistic way and added a glob of tomato sauce for a bit of colour. Then I took a mouthful and said, 'Mmmm! That is deeeeelicious!' as every TV chef does. End of programme. Let the credits roll . . .

Kaz came into the kitchen and ruined the moment. 'Talking to yourself?' she said.

'No,' I said and stuffed my mouth with Farmer Ben's Big Beef Sausages so I couldn't answer any more daft questions.

Kaz didn't fancy the sausages. She got a lettuce leaf out of the fridge. Typical. That meant I had to eat her share.

As I put the last chips into my mouth, I realised that 'Star Trek' had started – so I made a dash for the living room and pressed the remote. Before I settled down to watch, I noticed a car driving past very slowly. It was the black, American job with chrome bumpers.

79

'IT'S THEM!' I shouted. 'Come quick, Kaz! It's them!'

She came rushing in and we stared through the net curtains as the car disappeared up the road. Five minutes later, it came past again, this time the other way.

'They're trying to find Grandad's house,' I said.

'Why?'

''Cos they've found out we're here.'

'But we've got nothing to do with them.'

'You don't know the criminal mind, Kaz,' I said. 'We're connected with the bag. They'll probably torture us to make us talk!' I did one of my special hands-round-the-throat-tongue-sticking-out poses and she went into a panic.

'Don't be so stupid,' she said. 'They're probably not looking for us at all. They might be lost.'

My sister is so dim.

''Course they're looking for us. The diamonds from that robbery must be in that bag.'

Kaz looked worried. 'Probably...Yes...' She was biting her nails. Not even caring about her new nail polish – which just goes to show what a state she was in. 'We'd better switch off the telly,' she said.

'It's "Star Trek"!'

'And don't put any lights on.'

'Why?'

'We want them to think there's no one in. Right?'

'Right.'

I thought her idea was OK. But I had a plan of my own which was even better. This was it:

Collect rubbish from the bin under the sink – used tea

bags, potato peelings, leftover food – anything smelly and messy and slimy.

Fill a bucket with water and put all the rubbish in it.

Take upstairs and leave on the landing.

This plan was my protection in case they tried to break in.

Once I'd put the bucket in position, we waited. Nothing happened for ages. There was no telly to watch, or anything. Just Kaz moaning on about how she was missing her date with Jason. She was explaining the details of her love life (embarrassing, or what?), when there was a knock at the front door.

Knock! Knock! Knock!

We didn't say a word. We just froze on the spot, waiting to see what happened next. The knocking came again. Louder this time.

KNOCK! KNOCK! KNOCK! KNOCK! KNOCK! KNOCK!

'It might not be them,' Kaz hissed. Anyway, we thought it would be a good idea to go upstairs. So we did and we sat on the top step, watching the door and scared that it might burst open at any minute.

Then somebody called through the letterbox, 'Anybody home?'

It was the little fat bald guy I'd pushed down the stairs yesterday. I could tell by his voice.

'Let me try, Mickey,' said the other one and he shouted down the hall. 'OPEN UP OR YOU'RE IN DEAD TROUBLE.'

Pause.

'Ain't nobody in,' we heard him say.

'We'll break the door down, eh, Tone?'

'I'll do it, Mickey. Don't want you smashing up your other arm.'

It was just like Friday night all over again. But this time I had my emergency plan. I ran along the landing, grabbed the bucket and pushed the window open.

Tone and Mickey were standing below on the front step, both dressed in black (except for the white sling on Mickey's arm).

'Hey!' I called down and they both stepped back and looked up at me.

SPLASH! SLOP!

One bucket of stinking slops went out of the window. Bang on target. Nice one.

'Aaaaaaaagh!' screamed Tone (the thin one with two good arms). He got the worst of it – but Mickey's sling was now stained brown and covered in stinking tea leaves. If they'd had any sense, they'd have gone home to get cleaned up – but not Tone and Mickey. They went ballistic.

'Right, yer little sod!' Tone yelled. 'We'll show yer!'

My plan hadn't exactly worked. I was probably about to be captured and dragged away by two mad men.

Mickey and Tone ran at the door and smashed into it with their shoulders. (Ouch! Painful!) But the door was really solid and nothing happened. They stepped backwards, ready to have another go, when a taxi pulled up outside.

'Oy! You two!' someone shouted as the passenger door was flung open. 'What in blue blazes do you think you're up to, eh?'

It was Grandad.

'Grandad!' I shouted down. 'They're trying to break in.'

Grandad was really mad. 'Clear off,' he yelled, waving his crutch. 'Or I'll call the police.'

By then, the driver had run round the front of the taxi to see what was going on. He was fearsome. A cross between a rugby prop and a sumo wrestler.

'Clear off!' he yelled, 'or you hooligans will have me to deal with.' And he raised his large, tattooed fists towards them.

Mickey and Tone must have been terrified. They had their backs pressed against the door and were outnumbered, two to one (counting us upstairs). The only thing was to run for it.

It's a pity that Tone didn't notice Grandad's plastered leg poking out of the taxi. As he ran, he tripped right over it and went crashing to the pavement. SPLAT! I've never heard a man scream before. It was very loud. He must have been in terrible pain. Oh dear! What a shame!

'I think your arm needs medical attention,' said the taxi driver, pulling him to his feet. 'I'll run you to the hospital, if you like. It won't cost you much.'

I thought it was a very kind offer but Tone didn't take him up on it. I don't know why.

When Mickey and Tone had gone and the taxi had driven away, Grandad hobbled into the house.

'What a fight, eh?' I said. 'Better than the OK Corral.'

Grandad grinned and settled in his chair. Kaz fetched him a cup of tea and some extra thick chocolate Hob Nobs.

'Well, am I glad to be back!' Grandad said. 'They made a terrible fuss at the hospital, you know – but I said I wanted to go home to my family. I told them that there's nothing wrong with me that a few weeks of rest won't cure.'

'Glad you did, Grandad,' I said and helped myself to a couple of biscuits as there were several on the plate.

'Sure, I didn't feel comfortable leaving you on your own. I wanted to be here to make sure you were safe. Silly old man that I am.'

'You saved us,' said Kaz and gave him one of her mega hugs. Doesn't she ever consider his lungs could be damaged?

When he came up for air, he grinned at us. 'I'm looking forward to sleeping in my own bed tonight,' he said, 'and no one's going to wake me up in the morning to give me a bed bath.'

I agreed. Being forced to wash is a terrible thing.

He went to bed early that night. You should have seen him go up those stairs – backwards, sitting on his bum and pushing on his good leg. What a trooper!

When I went to bed, I got out my exercise book and wrote chapter 9.

# CHAPTER 9

Once Redwon had eaten the chocolate the girl had given him, his strength returned, as he knew it would. It was a pity this could not be said of the girl who still lay on the floor where she had fallen.

'Before we get moving,' he said, 'I need to look at the printout I got from the Black Serpents' computer.' He spread it out at the checkout and leaned over to study it.

'Look here! It even gives directions to where they're holding your father,' he said. 'Don't you think that's interesting?'

But Starlight didn't answer. She was jumping up and down and pointing towards the open door. 'Redwon! Redwon!' she squealed. 'Look out there! It'th thoth nathty Kwill people!'

Redwon looked up. His little sister was right. Across the road, walking out of The Blacksmith and Nail, was none other than Omph, the leader of the Krill Gang. And with him was his brother, Ilk.

'No sweat, Starlight,' he said, trying to calm her. 'They don't know we're here. Stay cool until they've gone.'

It was bad luck that, after a drinking session

at The Blacksmith and Nail, Omph had an irresistible urge to eat cabbage and custard flavoured crisps. The supermarket was the only shop in town to stock such a delicacy, and so Omph headed across the road, with Ilk following behind. As they walked through the doors, the first thing they saw was Redwon.

'Thrumpt! Thrumpt!' yelled Omph, waving his fists in the air. 'Ahhhgh – zooool!'

Redwon didn't hang around. He grabbed hold of Starlight and tore out of the fire exit. Once outside, he took off and flew a couple of miles to the wood just outside the town.

'We're safe here,' said Redwon. 'Now we'll plan our route to rescue your father. Pass me the paper, Starlight.'

'I don't have it, Thuperhewo,' she said.

'You don't?' said Redwon.

'I think it'th thtill in the thupermarket.'

He couldn't believe that the child had left it lying there. How careless is that? Now he had no idea which way to go. They would just have to spend the night in the wood and hope that, by morning, he had thought of a way to solve the problem.

Using his superhero muscle power, Redwon tore limbs from the trees and with swift karate chops, turned them into logs. By doing this, he made a comfortable cabin, brilliantly camouflaged, so that no one in a million years would be able to see it there among the undergrowth.

After all his hard work, Redwon took a stroll in the wood.

'Aaaaahhh!' he said as he breathed in the cool night air.

But as he did, his nostrils twitched. What was that unusual smell? he wondered. Cheesy Whatsits? No. Puffa Nibbles? Definitely not! The smell was like crisps – though not the normal kind.

Redwon couldn't work it out. He was standing there pondering when he suddenly heard a loud burp from behind some bushes – BRERRRR – and a gravelly voice said, 'Preing' (which means pardon me!).

Redwon turned ice cold. Someone was out there and it could only be his deadly enemies, the Krill brothers. Were they looking for him? How had they guessed he was here? He had to get back to the cabin and hide.

# Chapter 10

Grandad slept late the next morning. Kaz and I were having breakfast in front of the telly when the doorbell rang.

'Who's that?' I said.

'Postman,' said Kaz, heading for the door.

I didn't think so. I had this tingling in my spine which comes from years of studying criminal activities. 'Wait!' I hissed. 'It might be one of them.'

Kaz stood still.

'Who?'

'*Them!*'

'Why?'

'Criminals come back to the scene of the crime.'

'What scene?'

'Don't ask, Kaz. Check it out.'

We went over to the living room window and looked out. But couldn't tell who was standing there because of the porch. We could see a bit of a leather jacket – so we knew that it wasn't the postman.

'What now?' asked Kaz.

'I've got an idea. Listen to this.'

I used my impersonation of Mr Dobbin, our headmaster (which is well known in my class) and called down the hall. 'Who's that? If you're selling something, I'm not interested.' Whoever was at the door would never think there were just two defenceless kids in the house. Smart move, eh?

We waited and the letterbox flap rattled. Then it was pushed open and a voice called out, 'Hi, Max. It's Craig.' (I was miffed that he guessed it was me.)

Kaz squealed, 'It's Jamie's mum's boyfriend! You know. He has the designer clothes and the car!'

I was relieved it was Craig – but why would he come here? I opened the door and there he was on the doorstep. His car was parked in the road (a sporty silver job – very nice).

He stood, smiling. 'I hope you don't mind,' he said. 'I thought you could do with some help. Jamie told me about your problem.'

'Cool,' I said. 'Come in if you want.'

I took him into the living room. Kaz sat next to him on the sofa, all wide-eyed and trying to look grown-up.

'How's your grandad?' Craig asked. 'And, more to the point, how are you managing?'

'We're fine,' she said. 'I can look after Max OK. Do the cooking. That kind of thing.'

Do the cooking? What a cheek, I thought. The nearest thing to cooking that Kaz had done was wash a lettuce leaf.

'Anyway,' she said, 'Dad will be back later.'

'Oh, will he?'

'Yes, he had to work today. He's so busy these days. But he'll be back sometime this afternoon.'

All of a sudden, Craig looked really embarrassed and

stared at the floor. He was fidgety and kept twisting his fingers – a sure sign of nerves, if you ask me.

'Look,' he said. 'It's no good beating about the bush. I've got to tell you that I know what's happened to your dad.'

You should have seen Kaz's face. She turned bright red because she'd been caught lying through her teeth. I bet she wanted to burrow into the earth and crawl away like a worm down a worm hole.

'How did you find out?' I asked. 'We didn't tell anybody.'

He shook his head. 'I've got contacts down at the station. That's why I came. I thought you might need a bit of support. I don't know what happened but…'

'You'll never believe it,' I said. 'Two guys broke into our house. It was dead exciting! They were looking for the bag.'

'Max!' snapped Kaz. 'Keep quiet!'

I squeezed my lips together. I shouldn't have said anything.

'Don't worry, Kaz. I won't breathe a word,' said Craig, 'but I think you'd better tell me what's going on.'

We told him the whole story. It was a relief really. Dad's arrest. The thugs. The bag with diamonds in it (probably). And, last of all, our miraculous escape.

'Dad didn't have anything to do with the robbery,' I explained. 'But we can't go to the police yet. Dad told us not to.'

Craig was fantastic. He sat and listened to every word.

I think he was quite impressed by the way we'd coped.

'You kids have been through a lot, haven't you? It sounds to me as if you're in a dangerous situation. There's no knowing what lengths they'll go to if they want those diamonds.'

'So what do we do?'

'Come home with me. The bag can go in my safe.'

'Really?'

'Really.'

'You mean stay at your house with Jamie?'

He nodded.

'Oh yeah! Can I sleep in the top bunk?'

I'd always wanted to sleep in the top bunk. Craig grinned.

Going to Jamie's was a long way from the roller-coaster ride of the criminal world – not boring, exactly. But calm. Calm would be good, I thought.

Then Grandad walked in.

'And who's this then?' he grunted and we had to explain. He wasn't in the best of moods – I suppose his leg was a bit painful – but once we'd introduced him to Craig, he became quite civilised. They got on fine. Craig was a friendly kind of bloke. And when I said I was going to stay with Jamie, Grandad didn't mind. In fact, he thought it was a good idea.

'I'm not going, Grandad,' said Kaz. 'He can go if he wants to. I'm staying here to look after you. I won't leave you on your own.'

'That's grand, sweetheart,' he said. 'Thank you.'

I didn't have a problem with that. A few days on my own with Jamie would be great. I didn't waste any more time. I went upstairs and got the bag.

'Be good,' said Kaz as we walked out of the house. 'I'll give you a ring when I hear from Dad.'

'OK,' I said but I knew that I'd find out about Dad before she did. It was Craig who had the contacts.

I'd never been in a car like Craig's. It was really impressive – all leather seats and a racing gear stick. I sat in the front and – when the traffic allowed – we went quite fast. Craig even let me try out the CD player. Wicked!

Before I knew it, we were in Streatham, pulling up at 34 Hanover Road which was three times as big as our house with a garden and everything. I was gobsmacked. How could Jamie be this lucky?

As we walked into the hall, he was coming down the stairs.

'Hi, Jamie!' I said. 'Craig told me I could stay. Isn't it brilliant?'

But he didn't look all that pleased to see me and I wondered if he was mad with me for missing the practice. Maybe Old Bagsy put the blame on him.

'Show Max where he's going to sleep, Jamie,' Craig said. 'I expect he wants to see your bedroom.'

'Can I have the top bunk?' I asked, then wished I hadn't because when Jamie's in a funny mood, you don't ask questions. I should have waited.

'Leave the bag, Max,' said Craig. 'I'll put it in the safe in my office.'

'Cool!' I said. 'I don't know anybody with their own safe. Can I see it?'

He took me into his office, which was near the front door, and showed the safe. It was hidden behind a picture. Nobody would know it was there.

'Cor!' I said. 'It's just like a James Bond film.'

Craig laughed and put the bag inside. 'Yep!' he said. 'And only James Bond and me would be able to open it. Are you happy about that now?'

I was. Dad would be glad that nobody could get the bag. When he was released, he'd tell us what to do.

'Right then, Max. You go with Jamie. I think he wants to show you his laptop.'

My jaw dropped for the second time in five minutes. It seemed that Jamie had everything. I was about to follow him upstairs when I remembered the trip to EuroDisney. This was the perfect opportunity to work on Craig and angle for an invitation. I'd show him what amazing company I was and make him realise that he wanted me to join them on their holiday.

'You like jokes don't you, Craig?' I said.

'Yeah. Sometimes.'

'Have you ever heard the one about a cow with three legs?'

I think I must have told it to him before. He smiled but it didn't get much of a laugh. Win some, lose some. I'd try again later.

Jamie showed me his bedroom.

'Wicked!' I said.

It was huge with a big window overlooking the garden. There was a massive desk with a computer on it, a ginormous wardrobe and bunk beds against the wall. It was fantastic!

'It's OK,' said Jamie, 'but I'd rather have my old one.'

I couldn't believe what I was hearing. Had Jamie gone bananas or what?

'You're joking! Your old one was minute. Why?'

He sat on the edge of his bed and looked down at his feet. 'I don't like it because I don't like Craig.'

'What?'

'I wish we didn't live here. He's some kind of criminal.'

'That's crazy. Craig came to help us.'

'You don't know him. He's a thug.'

I couldn't get my head round this.

'You're saying he's a thug and yet you told him where Kaz and me were staying? It doesn't make sense.'

Jamie looked at me, shaking his head like mad. 'I didn't tell him! Honest! He tried to make me but I don't even know where your grandad lives.'

'Then how did he find out?'

Jamie shrugged and said nothing. I couldn't understand it. My mind was a blank until I suddenly realised what had happened.

After I'd talked to Craig on the phone (about the football practice), he must have dialled 1471. That way he got Grandad's phone number. Then he made someone ring us and pretend they were from the hospital. That's when we gave them the information about Grandad. The address and everything. Wow! It was brilliant. Simple but brilliant!

When it had all sunk in, panic struck. 'He's got the bag in his safe,' I said, leaping to my feet. 'We've got to get it back!'

'We're not going to get it back,' said Jamie.

'But the diamonds are in it somewhere. I know they are.'

'No,' said Jamie. 'There's nothing important in that bag.'

I stared at him and sank back on the bed. 'What?'

'Remember on Friday when I came to your house to show you my new gear?'

'Yes.'

'I picked up the wrong bag. They were both black, remember.'

It turned out that he'd taken the one Dean Holland left in the car, by mistake. To prove it, Jamie went over to the wardrobe and pulled out a sports bag. It was almost identical to the one I had put in Dad's room. He dumped it on the bed and he tipped out the contents: a couple of grubby towels, a shirt and a small cloth bag. I grabbed hold of the little bag, opened the cord at the top and emptied the contents onto the duvet. I could hardly believe it. Diamonds. Real, sparkling diamonds! I'd never seen anything like them.

At that minute, Craig called up the stairs. 'Jamie! Just come down a minute, will you?'

Jamie was gone for a quarter of an hour or more. So, not wanting to waste an opportunity, I quickly wrote chapter 10.

95

# CHAPTER 10

Redwon hurried back to the cabin. All that night, he and Starlight sat huddled together, hoping that the Krill brothers would not stumble on their hiding place. Then, as dawn broke, there was a loud knocking at the door – KNOCK! KNOCK! KNOCK! KNOCK! KNOCK! KNOCK! – which was a bit excessive in such a small place and gave Redwon a terrible headache.

'Who'th that?' whispered Starlight, shivering with fright and clinging to Redwon's leg.

'Do not be afraid, little one,' he said. 'I will protect you.'

He grasped his sword, strode across to the door and fearlessly flung it open. He had expected the deadly Krill brothers but, to his surprise, it was not. It was the Purple Knight. Redwon had met him before at a civic barbecue. He was quite a dashing local figure, well known for his designer armour, usually enamelled with fantastic colours and edged in gold. (He didn't go in much for silver.) Redwon looked up at him, totally impressed. He was sitting astride an amazing horse – pure white with a go-faster stripe across its girth.

'New horse?' Redwon said casually.

'This year's model,' said the Purple Knight.

'Lucky you,' said Redwon. 'Won't you come in?'

'Thank you, but no,' the Knight said. 'I was passing through the wood, and I saw your cabin. Maybe you would like to come and stay in my castle for a day or so? Underfloor heating – the lot. No one should be living in a shack like this.'

To be honest, Redwon was a bit offended at his cabin being called a shack – but the offer of a stay at the Purple Knight's castle was not to be sniffed at.

'OK. Thanks,' said Redwon, 'but I have to tell you that someone is hanging around in the wood. I think they're after me. There's no way I can walk out of here.'

The Purple Knight looked shocked. 'Someone hanging around? No, that can't be. I own these woods and we have CCTV coverage.'

But as he spoke, the Krill brothers, followed by three members of the gang, suddenly dashed out from their hiding places. They came screaming and howling and whooping.

'Thrumpt! Thrumpt! Ahhhgh – zooool!'

It was terrifying. Even the Purple Knight looked scared.

'I will save you,' said Redwon and he grasped the horse's reins in one hand and his sister's hand in the other. Up he rose, taking the Purple

Knight and Starlight with him, his cloak flapping like a ship's sail in the breeze.

Down below, the Krill Gang stood angrily shaking their fists as they watched their quarry escape yet again.

# Chapter 11

Jamie came back upstairs. 'I hate him,' he said. 'I don't know what Mum sees in him. Why did we have to come and live here?'

Jamie was really upset. Craig must have said something – but he wouldn't say what. He just said he'd prove to everybody that Craig was a crook.

I couldn't understand it. No wonder. I was dangerously hungry and incapable of thinking straight. Luckily, Jamie's mum came to the rescue.

'Are you boys ready for lunch?' she called up the stairs.

Even as I opened the bedroom door, the smell of chips drifted up from the kitchen and flooded my nostrils. I was downstairs in a flash.

'Knives and forks, please, Max,' said Jamie's mum.

I didn't mind setting the table. I liked to help. I got the tomato ketchup and HP sauce as well. (A thoughtful touch.)

She was cooking my favourite meal of sausages, bacon, eggs, home-made chips. She was doing it just for me. What a star!

'Haven't seen you for ages, Max,' she said standing at the cooker shaking the chip basket. 'I've almost forgotten what you like to eat.'

As she turned round to look at me, I noticed there was

something different about her. Her gorgeous blue eyes had lost their twinkle and she looked really old. Not Grandad-kind-of-old but . . . old. It was probably because she was living with that slimeball Craig. She would have been better to choose my dad. He would have made her happy. She would have enjoyed being with Dad and she could have cooked for me every day. I bet she'd like that.

Jamie slid into the chair opposite me without saying a word. He just tapped his mouth with his finger and gave me a funny look. Sort of 'don't mention the diamonds' kind of expression. 'Course I wouldn't dream of it. I'm not stupid. We didn't want Jamie's mum involved in criminal activity. She probably didn't have a clue that Craigy-boy was a bad-'un. It was so easy for him to lay on the charm and convince people he was a kind sweet guy – I don't think!

'Right,' said Jamie's mum. 'It's ready, boys.'

She put our plates in front of us and I dug in. She seemed really pleased that I was there. Maybe she'd missed me. She didn't mention Dad – but hey! His problems would soon be sorted. He'd be out of prison and then things would turn around. She'd realise what a mega mistake she'd made in choosing Craig.

'And what are you two doing this afternoon?' she asked as she passed me a slice of bread. (I didn't like to waste that runny yolk on the plate.)

'We thought we'd chill out in my room,' said Jamie. 'I want to show Max my new computer game.'

'Sound!' I said. And, as soon as we'd finished, we

went upstairs. I felt good. I had had a great meal and my brain was beginning to tick over.

Once we were by ourselves, we discussed what we should do. 'Got any ideas, Max?' Jamie asked.

'Sure.'

'What?'

'We'll hide the diamonds.'

It might sound crazy but wait till you've heard the master plan. First we went into Craig's bedroom and fished one of his dirty socks out of the clothes basket. Phew! What a stink! He should do something about those feet.

Then we tipped all the diamonds out of the bag into the sock.

Jamie was a bit puzzled, so I had to explain. 'The sock's covered in his DNA, see.'

I knew all about DNA and how you could track down criminals. I knew loads through watching detective series on TV. It was an obvious ploy.

The bathroom was the place for the next bit. We took a screwdriver and undid the panel from the side of the bath. It was a brilliant place for hiding things. In less than ten minutes the diamonds were stashed away and the panel was screwed back on.

After that and for the rest of the afternoon, we watched Craig's every move. We even stayed close while he talked to Jamie's mum in the kitchen and when he said that he was going out, we guessed that something was happening. We followed him to his study, pressed our ears against the door and heard him open the safe. When he came out, he was carrying a large plastic bag (obviously the sports bag was hidden inside it). He almost bumped into us and he looked dead guilty.

'Going shopping?' Jamie asked, all innocent.

'No, I'm just taking a package over to Brixton,' he said. 'I'm coming straight back so I'll have a game of football with you after. OK?'

He was acting Mr Nice Guy again.

'A package?' I said.

'Yes. I promised a friend I'd drop it over. I'll be back in a flash.'

He went out of the front door but I was too quick for him.

'I'll come with you for the ride, Craig,' I said as calm as you like. 'I think your car's really cool.'

'Er... it's rather important. It's business.'

'I thought you were just dropping something off?' I said.

You should have seen the look on his face. He could hardly hide the panic.

'Well, I . . .'

'Great,' I said, ran out to the car and jumped in before Craig had left the house.

Jamie followed. 'Might as well come too,' he said and climbed into the back seat.

'OK then,' muttered Craig (who didn't look at all pleased). 'But neither of you gets out of the car at Brixton. You stay put. Right?'

'Right,' I said.

'Right,' said Jamie and winked.

Once we were in Brixton, we went off the High Street and down narrower roads until we came to Waterloo Terrace where Craig pulled up at a house that looked a lot like Grandad's – but bigger. It was number 12.

He switched off the engine and climbed out of the car. 'Don't move!' he said looking directly at us. Then he slammed the door and pressed the key fob. THUNK. We were locked in. What a cheek.

We watched him walk up to number 12 and knock. The door soon opened and a large man with tattoos up his arm stood on the step.

'Hey, Craig. How you doin'? Got the gear at last. Good man.' He held out his hand, expecting Craig to pass him the plastic bag, but he hung onto it.

'I need to give it to the Boss,' Craig said.

'He's on his way from the airport,' said the tattooed man. 'He'll be half an hour or so. I'll give it to him.'

Craig hesitated but then another two men appeared behind the first one. Guess what? It was Tone and Mickey. One had his left arm in a sling, the other one now had his right arm in a plaster. Oh dear. What a shame.

'You'd better pass the goods over, Craig,' Mickey growled. 'The Boss has been waiting for this. He won't be pleased if they're not here when he gets back.' Then he stepped forward and snatched the bag out of Craig's grasp. 'You're acting like you don't trust us.'

The tattooed man laughed and slapped Craig on the

back. 'Stay cool, man,' he said and followed Mickey and Tone into the house.

'Which one was your friend, Craig?' I asked as he climbed back into the car. But he wasn't in the mood to answer. He just turned the ignition key and headed for home, his lips pressed tight together in a horrible grimace.

I relaxed in the back seat, pulled out my exercise book and concentrated on chapter 11.

# CHAPTER 11

The Purple Knight's castle was sensational – a swimming pool, a gym and rooms big enough to roller-skate in. But Redwon soon realised that they had been fooled. Things were not as they seemed.

For a start, the Purple Knight was not the gallant warrior everyone thought he was. No. He turned out to be a real bad lot. He had promised Redwon a decent room with TV, fridge, crisps and chocolate and en-suite facilities. That had been a total lie. Instead, he and Starlight were taken up to the tenth floor of the grim east wing and left to starve in a room which was cold, damp and bare, except for a skeleton hanging on the wall.

As if that wasn't bad enough, Redwon's cloak, helmet and sword were taken away – which meant that he had lost his magical powers. It was obvious. They had fallen into a trap.

All that day, they lay on the stone floor weak with hunger, then, as the sun rose the next morning, the Purple Knight burst in.

Redwon noticed he was wearing new stainless steel armour trimmed with pearls round the cuffs and the latest leather boots. But Redwon refused to comment on them. It was sheer extravagance.

The Knight swaggered into the room. 'I know you have the Jewels of Jaybal,' the Knight said. 'And I want them. Tell me where you have hidden them.'

'No way,' said Redwon, leaping to his feet.

'We shall see about that,' the Knight jeered. 'I have ways of making you talk.' He threw his head back and laughed a manic, mocking laugh, then he walked out of the room, slamming the door behind him.

He could have stayed for more of a conversation, Redwon thought. It was hardly worth the effort of climbing all those stairs.

Starlight was terrified. 'What will happen now?' she sobbed. 'Ith he going to kill uth? I'm fwightened.'

'Stay cool,' said Redwon, putting his arm around her shoulder. 'I won't let that purple monster get you.'

She looked up at him adoringly and sighed.

But if Redwon thought that beating the Purple Knight was going to be easy, he was wrong. The Knight had some very trixy plans up his designer sleeves, which our superhero was about to discover.

While Redwon was wondering what he could do, he noticed that the stone floor of the room was beginning to shake. Gently, like blackcurrant jelly at first, then, after a loud rumbling below, the floor started to tremble so violently that Redwon and Starlight had to hold onto the wall.

'What'th happening?' sobbed the little girl.

Redwon shook his head. He didn't know either.

Cracks were appearing in the slabs and Redwon saw them split wide open.

But it was Starlight who saw what was inside the cracks. She screamed, 'Aaaaaaaaaaaaagh!' and pointed to the far corner.

Redwon turned to look. Out of the stone the heads of blood red scorpions were appearing. Next came their tentacles and then their stinging tails. Dragging themselves out of the cracks, they scuttled across the floor. There were dozens of them – hundreds. Vicious, poisonous things. And they were heading towards the captives.

'Mmm,' said Redwon. 'This could be tricky.'

# Chapter 12

My plan was working well so far. By going to Brixton with Craig, we'd found out where the Boss-man lived. The Godfather. The Numero Uno criminal behind the diamond robbery. The police would be dead impressed with this information.

Since we'd been back, Craig was in a seriously bad mood. He had been prowling around the house like a bear with toothache. He didn't know what to do with himself. One minute he was looking at his watch, the next he was checking his mobile. Over and over. He looked really nervous but we pretended not to notice.

'We're off to the common, Mum,' Jamie called into the living room. 'We're taking the football. OK?'

'OK, darlin',' his mum called back. 'Be home for tea, won't you?'

No problem! We weren't going to miss the downfall of Crooked Craig. No way.

Going to the common was just a cover story. We were really heading towards the town because we needed to find a phone box.

'There's one,' I said as we turned the corner. 'Got the money?'

Jamie handed over several coins. 'Glad you're doing this,' he said. 'You're better at voices than I am.'

True. I was pretty good at imitating teachers –

although I was still upset that Craig hadn't been fooled by my Mr Dobbin impression.

We both squeezed into the phone box.

'Right,' said Jamie. 'Here's the number.'

He pulled a screwed-up piece of paper from his pocket. Written across it in black biro was the number of the local police station.

'Right,' I said. I pushed a coin in the slot and tapped out the number.

'Hello,' I said in a Brummy voice. This was my Mr Bradshaw imitation. (He's my class teacher and comes from somewhere near Birmingham.) 'I've got some information for you about the Hatton Garden diamond robbery.'

'Your name, sir?'

'Sorry, can't tell you,' I said cunningly. 'I'm working under cover.'

'James Bond, are we, sir?'

'No, but I'm here to give you top secret information.'

'Right.'

'Go to 34 Hanover Road, you'll find the stolen diamonds.'

'Oh yes?'

'Yes. Under the bath.'

'The bath?'

'Yes. They're in a sock.'

'Very unusual, sir.'

'Go now and you'll catch the crook, too.'

'Will I?'

'Yes, he's there right now.'

'This is a joke, isn't it?'

My jaw dropped. Had the police sunk this low?

'A joke?' I gasped. 'No, it certainly isn't a joke. Maybe the police would catch more criminals if they took information more seriously.' And I slammed the receiver down. Honestly!

'That was cool,' said Jamie. 'Pity about the last bit.'

'What?'

'You forgot to change your voice.'

Oh well. Everybody makes mistakes sometimes.

After that, I rang Grandad and Kaz to tell him about Craig.

'But we've got it sussed, Grandad,' I said. 'We've got a fantastic plan and it's already in action. We should be able to clear Dad's name by tonight.'

Grandad asked loads of questions. He was probably worried – what with Craig being a major criminal and that. Then Kaz came on the phone with even more questions.

'Got to go,' I said. 'My money's running out.'

As we left the call box, the skies clouded over and it started to rain. This was a bit of luck because now we could go back to Hanover Street without anybody being suspicious.

'We're back, Mum,' Jamie called when we walked through the door. 'We were rained off.'

His mum was in the living room with Craig. 'That's a shame,' she said. 'You were so keen to practise. Maybe you could go later if it stops.'

'I think we'll watch TV for a bit,' Jamie said and plonked himself on the sofa between his mum and Craig.

Craig was pleased – I don't think. He gave Jamie's mum a terrible look. 'Can't they go upstairs?' he said. 'Jamie's got his own TV.'

'Too small,' said Jamie who was feeling brave. 'This one's much better.' He beckoned me to sit next to him (which was a bit of a squash and annoyed Craig even more).

'OK, sweetheart,' Jamie's mum said and handed him the remote. 'Stay down here if you want.'

Just as the telly came on, Craig's mobile rang. 'Hello,' he said.

Pause.

'What? No I didn't.'

Pause.

'What? Say again.' He glowered at Jamie. 'Turn the sound down, can't you?'

Jamie immediately pressed the volume switch – the wrong way. Just a mistake, you understand.

Craig stood up and marched into the hall where it was quieter. We put the volume down so we could hear what he was saying and peered over the top of the sofa to watch. Craig was turning an interesting shade of blood pressure red.

'I tell you it's those ghouls of yours,' he shouted. 'You can't trust them. They must have taken them.'

Then the doorbell rang.

'I'll get it,' said Jamie.

111

We both leapt off the sofa, pushed past Craig and opened the front door. It was the police. My plan was working brilliantly.

'Good afternoon, boys,' said a tall policeman with a large, black moustache. 'Is your dad in?'

'No, he isn't,' said Jamie, 'but Craig is. Come in.'

Craig was standing at the foot of the stairs still absorbed in his phonecall. But when he looked up and saw the police he went deathly pale and flipped the lid of his mobile shut.

'What is it?' he said. 'What's wrong?'

'Nothing really, sir,' said the policewoman (plumpish with a nice smile). 'We've had this silly anonymous call. Probably kids. Said there were some stolen diamonds in this house.'

'What?' said Craig.

'Ridiculous, isn't it? Diamonds, they said.'

'Where?'

'Under the bath.'

Craig shook his head in disbelief. 'So it was a hoax call, officer. You must get hundreds of them. Forget it. I'm a very busy man.'

'We can't forget it, I'm afraid, sir. We have to follow it up. Regulations and all that.'

'So?'

'So I wonder if you'd mind if we looked under your bath?'

Craig laughed nervously. 'This is ridiculous. I don't believe it. Why would there be diamonds under my bath?'

'I know, sir. Kids, eh? Who'd have 'em? But if you wouldn't mind… We can clear the matter up quickly.'

Craig was in such a temper there was steam coming out of his ears. He stomped off towards the stairs muttering, 'This is ridiculous,' over and over. (I counted eight.)

The police followed Craig. Jamie's mum followed the police. We followed everybody. There was no way we were going to miss a thing.

# CHAPTER 12

The scorpions scurried across the floor. Hairy legs. Curled tails. Hard, shiny backs. Redwon, lying on the stone slabs, was powerless to stop them.

Starlight screamed again. 'Oh nooooooooooooo-ooooooo! We'll be poithoned!'

Redwon turned towards her. 'Got any pockets, Starlight?' he asked.

She nodded. 'Lotth.'

'Then dig into all of them and see if you can find some chocolate. Even a tiny piece will do. It's the only thing which will give me strength.'

Luckily, Starlight always went for clothes with pockets – the more the better – even in pyjamas. Although it took ages for her to feel into all of them, she finally found a piece of chocolate tucked away in a little pile of fluff.

'Ooooh!' she said, pulling it out. 'My favorwite!' and she was just about to pop it in her mouth when Redwon whipped it from her grasp.

'I need it,' he said, 'to get us out of here.'

No sooner had the chocolate melted on his tongue, than he felt his strength rushing through his veins. He took a deep breath and filled his lungs. Then he blew hard across the room like a violent tornado, sending the scorpions sliding back helplessly. No matter how the creatures tried, no matter how crazily they waved their legs, they couldn't stop. They slid until they reached the cracks in the floor, where they dropped and disappeared from sight.

'Oh, Redwon,' Starlight sighed. 'You have thaved uth. But how will we ethcape from this tewible plathe?'

Redwon rubbed his chin and suddenly remembered that the Purple Knight had not locked the door behind him when he left. Not only that, but just outside, at the top of the stairs, he found his cloak, helmet and sword abandoned on the floor.

'Two bad mistakes, Purple Knight,' he scoffed as he flung the cape over his shoulders and pulled on the helmet.

Then Redwon pointed up to a window – it was at least ten metres off the ground. 'We have to jump up there, Starlight,' he said. 'Do you think you can hang onto me?'

Starlight smiled. She knew Redwon wouldn't let her fall. But as she grabbed hold of his shoulders, she felt something sharp latch onto her leg. Something sharp, deadly and poisonous.

# Chapter 13

Jamie's mum was really worried. 'What's going on?' she kept saying as we all trooped up the stairs. We couldn't tell her, could we? We couldn't explain that the man she planned to live with for the rest of her life was about to get slung into prison. So we kept quiet and watched from the landing while the policeman unscrewed the panel off the side of the bath.

You should have seen Craig! He looked as though he was going to explode at any minute. He stood there with his arms folded, clenching his teeth.

'Why are you doing this?' he said. 'I'm a law-abiding citizen. I've never...'

He didn't finish his sentence because at that exact moment the policeman found what he was looking for under the bath. I nudged Jamie and he nudged me back. The policeman reached for the sock and pulled it out.

'Aha!' he said. 'And what have we here, sir?'

He opened the top of the sock and peered inside. Then he tipped the contents carefully onto the palm of his hand.

'Hello, hello, hello,' he said. 'Could these be diamonds? What do you think, constable?'

The policewoman leaned over and looked closely. 'Ooooh er, sarge, I think they might be diamonds. Blow me down and call me a sniffer dog. It wasn't a hoax call after all.'

By then Craig was a strange shade of purple and was spluttering like he'd forgotten how to speak. 'I...I...'

'What was that, sir?' said the policeman. 'Did you have something to say about this?'

Craig must have realised the game was up. He suddenly lunged forward and pushed the sergeant in the chest.

'Aggghhhh!' yelled the sergeant and he toppled backwards into the bath.

The policewoman couldn't help giggling. 'Oh, sarge,' she said. 'Taking a bath in police time!' We thought it was a good joke but the sergeant didn't. He was choking with rage.

'Quick, stop him!' he yelled as Craig dashed out onto the landing. Luckily we blocked his escape. Jamie, his mum and me. So Craig couldn't get through.

That didn't please him one little bit.

'Move out of the way, you stupid...' he yelled. 'I'm getting out of here.'

'You're not going anywhere,' said the policewoman, who was already behind him. She grabbed his arm and slapped handcuffs on him. She was pretty quick, I tell you. He didn't stand a chance.

But when Jamie's mum burst into tears, we were shocked. You'd think she'd be happy to see him brought to justice. But then I never understood women.

The sergeant struggled out of the bath and emerged from the bathroom, straightening his uniform and looking furious. They dragged Craig downstairs and there was a bit of a struggle in the hall – some shouting, too, as they tried to take him to the front door.

Before they reached it, the doorbell rang. Ringgggg.

Everybody was too busy to answer it.

It rang again. Ringgggggggg. Ringggggggggggggg.

Then a loud voice shouted. 'Don't pretend you're not in, you scumbag. I'll give you ten seconds to open up and then my men'll smash the door in. See how you like that.'

The two police officers stopped what they were doing and looked up. I have to say they looked quite worried. No wonder. They had left their radio in the car so they couldn't call for back-up. *

I decided it was up to me to save the situation. I quickly slipped into the kitchen. Then I dialled 999.

'Police, fire or ambulance?' the voice said.

'Yes please,' I said.

'Are you in trouble?'

You would think it was obvious. I wouldn't have dialled 999 if I wasn't.

'Send the police to 34 Hanover Street,' I said. 'Two coppers are being threatened by a gang of diamond robbers.'

I put the phone down and rushed back into the hall. The sergeant was trying to stop the thugs breaking the door down. 'I must warn you,' he called in a big, brave voice, 'we are the police. Do not try anything stupid, sir, or we will have to arrest you.'

'You and whose army?' the man shouted back through the letterbox. 'Ignore 'im, lads. Go for it.'

---

*Back-up is a technical term the police use for getting extra help. Not a lot of people know that.

118

There was a tremendous THWACK! BANG! as the henchmen ran full pelt at the door and it burst open. Bits of wood shot through the air and two thugs came flying into the hall like guided missiles, colliding head-on with Craig and the police. They all collapsed in a great heap on the floor where they stayed, thrashing about and cursing like a heap of bad-tempered crabs. That was when the Chief Thug appeared. He stepped carefully over the bodies and walked into the hall. I recognised him at once. It was Dean Holland.

'Get up, you stupid pair,' he growled at his men – who were none other than Tone and Mickey. (They seemed to crop up everywhere.) 'Tie up the coppers and let's take this lying toad away with us. I'll show him you can't cheat on me.'

This was not what I'd planned. I wanted Craig to be arrested and put in prison. I wanted to know he was behind bars like a real criminal. Now anything might happen. Craig might convince Dean Holland that someone had set him up. Dean Holland might even realise it was me who'd hidden the diamonds. He might come back to get me. Scary or what? I just hoped the back-up police would get here soon.

I looked at my watch.

Dean must have noticed. 'You got somewhere to go, kid?' he said.

I shook my head fiercely but he just sniggered.

'Don't worry,' he said. 'We'll soon be out of your way. Got a girlfriend somewhere, have yer?' Typical of the criminal mind.

Tone and Mickey, had almost finished tying up the police. (They did this quite well considering they had serious injuries to their arms.) I glanced at my watch again. The seconds were ticking away. Then I heard footsteps outside. The doorbell rang. SAVED!

'Who's that?' Dean Holland snapped at Craig.

'Dunno,' said Craig. At least I think that's what he said. It was hard for him to speak clearly – what with the pain of the handcuffs and being pushed around.

'Get him into the kitchen,' Dean Holland said and Tone and Mickey dragged Craig like a sack of spuds out of the hall. 'You as well, lady,' he said to Jamie's mum. 'Just leave the kids.'

Then Dean Holland turned to me and grabbed me by the scruff of the neck. He pressed his nose to mine (which was not pleasant on account of his terrible breath).

'Now you listen, kid,' he said. 'Go and answer the door. Right? Tell 'em your dad's not in. Nothing else. Then shut the door. Right?'

'Right,' I said. 'Shall I go now?'

'Hang on till I get into the kitchen,' Dean Holland said. 'Don't want anybody seeing me in here.' He slipped out of the hall and shut the kitchen door behind him.

'OK, kid. Do it – and do it right. Right?' he shouted.

The doorbell rang again.

'OK, I'm coming,' I called out and I turned the handle and pulled the door open.

But it wasn't the police.

It was Grandad and Kaz.

# CHAPTER 13

A terrible thing had happened. In spite of Redwon's powerful breath (which was better than any clean machine), not all the scorpions had been blown down the cracks in the stone floor. Two were swept into the corners where they stayed until Redwon and Starlight made the leap towards the window. Then they latched onto Starlight's legs as she wasn't wearing socks at the time.

'Noooooooooooooooooooo!' she screamed while the creatures clung on and stung like crazy.

But Redwon, who was amazingly brave, held Starlight with one hand and grabbed hold of the scorpions with the other – not caring about the pain and danger – and he flung them away. He watched as they slammed against the wall and fell down senseless. Even though Redwon was in terrible pain, he managed to hold on tight to his sister and take flight out of the window.

Away they went, leaving the Purple Knight's castle behind, until Redwon became aware that Starlight was hanging heavy and lifeless from his hand. He looked down and saw that her eyes were closed – a sure sign that the scorpions' poison was too strong for a kid. She was probably dying.

Desperate to save his sister, Redwon flew low over a valley searching the ground below with his superhero laser vision. He was looking for something special. He looked on the banks of the river, by boulders among the heather, until he came to the gentle slope of a small hillside – and there it was. A small golden flower.

'Yes!' he said and dived towards the ground. 'I've found the throgmirtle plant.'

He laid Starlight on the grass, picked the tiny flower and squeezed the nectar onto his sister's eyes.

'Aaaahhhh,' she moaned softly and her lids fluttered open.

'Saved!' said Redwon. 'Now I can take the throgmirtle plant to old Grandol. He will recover and help us find your father.'

Starlight smiled gratefully. 'Redwon,' she said. 'How can I ever thank you?'

# Chapter 14

There was Grandad at the door. He was the last person I expected to see. And as for my sister...

'Oh heaven be praised you're all right, Max!' Grandad said, standing with his crutches under his armpits. 'I've been worried to death. What on earth's going on, son?'

Kaz, who was behind him, pushed forward. 'I tried to get Grandad to stay at home but he phoned for a taxi.'

I flapped my hand at them and hissed, 'Go away! You'll ruin everything.'

I tried shutting the door but I couldn't stop them. Grandad charged in – well, limped really – and then he started shouting at the top of his voice like a wild man.

'WHERE'S THIS CRAIG FELLA?' He looked round the hall at all the closed doors. Then he shouted again. 'COME OUT, YOU WIMP, WHEREVER YOU ARE. KIDNAPPING MY GRANDSON. LET ME GET MY HANDS ON YOU!'

The kitchen door slowly opened.

'Ah, he's daring to show his face, so he is. Look, Max! He's coming. Well, he's in for some punishment, I tell you.'

I watched Grandad hobble down the hall and come face to face – not with Craig, as he thought – but with Dean Holland. The master criminal. The Godfather. And he was followed by Mickey and Tone.

'Who's this old fool?' growled Dean Holland.

'I'm Max's grandad. That's who,' said Grandad, poking the thug in the chest with his crutch. 'Just show me some respect, sonny, or I'll have your guts for garters, so I will.'

He poked him again and Dean Holland sprang forward with his fists raised ready to thump Grandad.

Kaz screamed, 'No!'

Dean Holland yelled, 'I'LL FIX YOU – YOU OLD GIT!'

Suddenly everything went crazy.

Grandad raised his crutches and whirled them round his head like a cowboy about to lasso a steer. Then sirens came blaring down the road EEE AAW EEE AAW EEE AAW and a jam doughnut screeched to a halt outside. Four doors were flung open and four policemen leapt out and ran in waving their batons. It was great! I've never seen so many people crammed into one hall.

In the end, all went well – although the police officers were not ace detectives. I suppose it was understandable that they thought Grandad was the criminal and arrested him. After all, he must have looked pretty fierce, swinging his crutches at Dean Holland who was on the floor, shouting, 'Get him off me!' and holding his arms over his head for protection. I had to take the police officer to one side and explain who the real villain was. When they realised their mistake, they apologised to Grandad, made him a cup of tea and arrested Dean Holland.

Of course, that was only the start. Next they arrested Tone and Mickey for brutality towards the police.

'Tying us up like that,' said the sergeant rubbing his bruised wrists. 'They deserve all they get.'

'Shouldn't be allowed, sarge,' said the policewoman.

After that, they arrested Craig.

Jamie's mum went berserk. 'How could you mislead me like that?' she screamed at Craig. 'Pretending to be so nice when you were just a rotten thug underneath.'

Then she slapped him across the head THUMP! THWACK! THUNK! with a cookery book that happened to be handy.

The police sergeant, once he'd recovered from being tied up, produced the sock he'd found earlier and held it out for the other officers to see. 'This was under his bath,' he said. 'It was hidden.'

'I'd hide mine if it smelled like that,' said one policeman.

'A dirty sock?' said another. 'I've got loads in my bathroom.'

'Not like this, mate,' said the sergeant. 'Diamonds hidden in this one.'

'Diamonds?'

'Yeah. Stolen from Hatton Garden.'

The policemen gulped.

'You mean that's the haul from the Hatton Garden robbery?'

The sergeant looked smug. 'Yeah,' he said. 'Not a bad result, eh?'

Soon a big black van arrived and the criminals were pushed inside. But the rest of us (the witnesses!) rode in real police cars. Pity they wouldn't switch the sirens on or drive at 90 miles an hour like they do in films. Even so, it was really cool.

Next stop: Streatham Police Station.

When we walked in, it was just like it is on the telly. The room with the table and chairs. The tape recording. The interviews. I don't have to tell you. You've seen it all before.

Two policemen asked us loads of questions but I was a bit miffed that Kaz did most of the answering at first.

'It's because I'm the oldest,' she said. 'You're too young to be a witness so I have to explain things as they were. They expect it.'

Cheek!

In spite of Kaz, I gave them loads of information. After all, I'd been there in the car with Craig AND I'd called 999 AND I'd saved the police from the clutches of Dean Holland and his murdering thugs. The police were dead impressed.

'I wouldn't be surprised if you get a medal,' said one of the officers. 'Smart work, son. You kept a cool head in very difficult circumstances.'

How's that for somebody too young to be a witness (sez Kaz!).

'By the way,' said the Inspector, 'I don't suppose you've got any ideas on catching the Streatham Park Flower Thief, have you? We'd appreciate your help.'

It was nice to be asked but, after thinking about it for at least two seconds, I had to decline.

Jamie's mum was really upset when she learned that she was living with a big-time criminal. 'Why didn't I realise he was such a lowlife?' she said. 'I put Jamie's life in danger. How could I?' And she burst into tears.

The Inspector stood up and put his arm round her. He pulled a hankie from his pocket, handed it to her and she blew her nose hard.

'Thanks,' she said and smiled up at him. (I hoped she hadn't taken a liking to the Inspector as I was keeping my fingers crossed that my dad was in with a chance now that Craig was finished.)

All in all, the police seemed really pleased with the information we gave them.

What happened next was this:

Craig grassed up* Dean Holland.

Dean Holland grassed up* Tone and Mickey.

Tony and Mickey grassed up* Craig and Dean Holland (when they got out of hospital following injuries sustained during the forced entry).

So they all told on each other. Fair's fair.

But I bet you're wondering about our dad and what was happening to him. He was still in nick, that's what.

I had a heart-to-heart with the Inspector. (We were good mates by then.) 'It's obvious he didn't do the

_____

*grassed up is a technical term which means you tell on your mates and get them into trouble. A detective would know such an expression and it's worth remembering.

robbery,' I said. 'Look at the facts. It's as clear as a cherry on a bath bun that he should be let out.'

'Yeah!' said Jamie.

'Yes,' said Jamie's mum. 'Let him go.'

Kaz smiled at the Inspector in a yucky girlie way and said, 'Pleeeze!'

Honestly! That girl can be so embarrassing!

Anyway, the Big Chief disappeared from the interview room and we waited and then...

In walked Dad.

# CHAPTER 14

Redwon and Starlight headed back to the White Witch's beer barrel. There they found Grandol lying on a wooden pallet, near to death.

'Leave him alone,' said the White Witch, quietly dragging on a cigar. 'Can't an old man die in peace?'

'Die? NO!' said Redwon and he waved the throgmirtle flower triumphantly under her nose. She was so amazed that her cigar fell onto the rug which caught fire.

'No sweat,' she said, stamping her boots on the flames. 'I'm insured.'

She picked up the flower in her hands, which were as dry and cracked as flaky pastry owing to a local shortage of hand cream.

'Well,' she said, 'I've not seen the throgmirtle flower these hundred years. Let's get the recipe book quick. It's on the bookshelf somewhere.'

The beer barrel was lined with bookcases all stuffed with ancient, leather-bound books (some of which had been borrowed from the local library and never returned). They searched until they found what they were looking for. How to Cure: book 2 by Amelia Smith (the book of the TV series).

'Hurry, before he snuffs it,' said the White Witch when she had turned to the right page. 'Get some toad's blood and mix it with the throgmirtle juice.'

They dashed out to the nearest pond and found a toad who didn't mind giving a drop of blood providing he had tea and biscuits afterwards.

The potion was one of Amelia Smith's best-loved recipes with a short cooking time. When it was ready and cooled, the thick, orange mixture was poured into Grandol's mouth through a funnel. This was a simple procedure, as he slept with his mouth wide open, and it worked immediately. In seconds, the old man sat bolt upright and ram-rod straight, like a jack-in-a-box whose spring has suddenly been released.

'Well, my dears,' he said. 'How nice to see you. Been doing anything interesting lately? Did you find that man you were looking for?'

At this Starlight burst into tears.

'She's upset,' said Redwon, showing the considerate side of his superior nature. 'Even though I am a superhero, I haven't been able to find her father, I'm afraid.'

'Dear, dear,' said Grandol. 'Well, we can't all be perfect. Follow me and I shall lead you to the place where he is being held. But don't hang about. I want to be home for tea.'

# Chapter 15

So what happened after the police raid?

Well, somehow the press found out about Dean Holland's arrest. When we walked out of the station there were dozens of flash bulbs popping and people shouting questions at us – wanting to know how we had helped in the downfall of a major crook. The next day there were headlines in the paper.

KIDS ESCAPE JEWEL THIEVES.
LOCAL BOY SOLVES DIAMOND ROBBERY.

A TV station interviewed me because it was my brilliant idea that broke up a notorious criminal gang. When they asked if I was going to join the police when I grew up, I said no. I was going to be a famous novelist and make loads of money. I told them I'd almost finished a book and they wanted to know all about it.

'I can't tell you,' I said. 'It's a secret. I'm saving it for a big launch in London.'

After Craig and the gang had been arrested, there was one problem. Jamie and his mum had nowhere to stay. She couldn't stay in the house of a well-known criminal, could she?

So Dad said, 'Stay with us, Katie – just till you find somewhere of your own, of course.'

Cool! Jamie could sleep in my bedroom and we'd be

able to talk till late. And we'd be able to go to school together and practise footie whenever we liked. I couldn't think of anything better.

Jamie's mum seemed pleased, too. 'That's so kind of you, Mark,' she said. 'I really appreciate it. How can I ever repay you?'

'You could do the cooking,' I said – which I thought was a reasonable suggestion at the time – but Dad gave me one of his frowns and shouted, 'MAX!'

I was only trying to help.

Anyway, she couldn't have thought it was such a bad idea because she did cook for us that night. Steak pie, chips and peas with apple crumble and custard to follow. Fantastic!

Grandad was impressed, too. 'She's a fine cook, so she is,' he whispered to me.

'I told you, didn't I, Grandad?'

'You did, son. So you did,' he said and then he looked directly at Jamie's mum.

'Sure, you'll make someone a wonderful wife, sweetheart. Would you consider taking on Mark here?'

'Grandad!' giggled Kaz.

'Dad!' shouted my dad.

But I said, 'I think that's a brilliant idea.' And Jamie agreed.

I don't know why Jamie's mum turned pink. I mean, it was quite a compliment, wasn't it? No need to be embarrassed about it. I think Dad should have jumped at the chance right there. Gone down on his knees or whatever, and asked her to marry him. It would have been dead romantic. But he didn't. He just muttered, 'I give up,' under his breath.

Grandad came to stay in our house, too. We couldn't let him live by himself with a broken leg, could we? Anyway, Grandad's great. We always have a good time together. He was going to sleep in Dad's room and Dad would sleep on the sofa.

'Right y'are,' said Grandad. 'It'll be good to stay. Just for a bit, mind! I'll have a flutter on the gee-gees while I'm convalescing. See if I can't make a nice little nest egg for you.'

'No gambling,' said Dad. 'It's a bad example to the kids.'

'All right, son,' he said and then he winked across at me.

Later, when we'd finished the washing up, we had a video from the shop – a film about invaders from an alien planet who turned everybody green and tried to take over the world. Fantastic! Kaz thought it was a bit juvenile so she went upstairs and phoned Jason.

We were allowed to stay up quite late that night. It was just after ten and we were all having a drink and some biscuits. I was on my third chocolate digestive when Dad came up with a real thunderbolt.

'I've got something to ask you, kids,' he said.

'What?' I said.

'Fire away,' said Kaz.

'How would you feel if we moved away from here?'

Wow! That was a shock and a half, if you like. I'd

lived in Streatham all my life. I didn't know anywhere else. And what about Jamie?

'Where would we go, Dad?'

'The country,' he said. 'I've had enough of traffic and criminals and thugs down every street.'

I thought this was a bit over the top. I hadn't met a single crook in Streatham until a few days ago. But, given Dad's recent experience, I understood why he said it.

'Do we have to?' Kaz whined. 'What about my friends. I won't see them if we go away.'

'You mean spotty Jazzo-boy?' I said. 'Good riddance, I say.'

I got a punch in the shoulder for that. My sister never could take a joke.

Jamie's mum smiled. 'I shouldn't worry, Kaz,' she said. 'Jason could always come and visit you. And you'll make new friends. New boys to meet. Lots of them.'

I could see Kaz could see that maybe it wasn't such a bad idea.

'Well, it's OK by me,' I said. 'But we can't go for another week. It's our football final and there's no way I'm going to miss that.'

Dad laughed. ''Course not. It will take time to find another house and sell this one.'

That was OK then.

Dad settled back in his chair. 'So you both agree that moving is quite a good idea then.'

Kaz nodded.

'I agree,' I said. 'But on one condition.'

'What's that?'

'Grandad has to come and...'

'If he wants to.'

'Oh aye,' said Grandad. 'That sounds grand – out in the country. We might even live near a racecourse. Wouldn't that be something, eh?'

'So that's settled,' said Dad.

'I haven't finished,' I said. 'I'll go on condition that Grandad, Jamie and his mum come too.'

It was a simple request. I don't know why Dad insisted that we went to bed right then without another word. 'Go now, Max! Now!' he kept saying. I suppose he wanted to think about it.

Just before we went to sleep, I said to Jamie, 'It's so brilliantly simple. All our problems will be solved if we all go together. Sooner or later, even my dad will see it makes sense.'

'Yeah,' said Jamie. ''Course he will.'

And he turned off the light.

I pulled the duvet over my head and switched on my torch. I needed to finish my novel and make mega bucks so we could buy a house in the country – big enough for all of us, with a football pitch at the back.

# CHAPTER 15

Redwon, Starlight and Grandol headed north. Little did they know that the Krill Gang had tracked them down. Little did they know that they were only half a mile behind. Even with his superior sense of smell, Redwon had failed to notice the aroma of cabbage and custard crisps. It was a serious mistake.

When they came to a steep rocky mountain capped in snow, Grandol pointed skywards. 'We must reach the summit,' he said. 'That is where Starlight's father is being held.' So they struggled to the top which was difficult for Grandol as his arthritis was playing him up something shocking.

At the highest point, Grandol suddenly stopped and flung his arms wide like an Old Testament prophet. 'Look yonder,' he cried in a quaking voice. 'The tree! The tree!'

On the top of a craggy rock stood a craggy old oak. Redwon and Starlight stopped in their tracks and stared. Suspended from the oak – hanging from the topmost branch – was a large wicker cage and inside was their father.

'You found him, Grandol!' said Redwon, but the old man couldn't speak. All that climbing and waving his arms about had taken his breath away.

But Starlight had plenty of breath. As soon as she saw her father, she started to scream.

'AAAAAAAAAAAGGGGGGGGGGGGHHHHHHHH!
AAAAAAAAAAAGGGGGGGGGGGGHHHHHHHH!
AAAAAAAAAAAGGGGGGGGGGGGHHHHHHHH!
AAAAAAAAAAAGGGGGGGGGGGGHHHHHHHH!'

She broke away from Redwon and ran towards the cage. 'DADDY!' she shouted, over and over. (Forty-eight times, to be precise.)

Of course, Redwon realised that the cage was a trick and shouted to warn her – but it was too late. Hiding behind the tree were the only Black Serpents in existence (Redwon had killed the rest earlier that week) – and they suddenly emerged, grinding their teeth and scaring Starlight out of her skin. Not only that, but the Krill Gang arrived from the other direction and joined in with their 'Thrumpt' and 'Zooool'. She didn't stand a chance. Before she knew it, she had been scooped up and slammed inside the cage.

Grandol, gasping for breath, turned to Redwon. 'There is nothing I can do for you,' he said. 'The climb up the mountain has weakened me. I have no power left.'

'No probs, Grandol,' said Redwon. 'I have a secret weapon.'

Pulling the thread, which held the magic cloak

together, he made a lasso. He whirled it round his head until it made a weird, wild, humming noise and took on a life of its own. Then it spun away and dropped on the deadly enemies massing under the cage. It wound round and round them, taking them completely by surprise and wrapping them in a giant cocoon.

Redwon ran across the hillside and called to Starlight and Dad. 'I'll cut you down now,' he said.

He pulled his Power Sword from its sheath and began to cut at the rope but, before he had finished, he heard the thunder of hooves. As the superhero turned and saw the Purple Knight heading towards him, he lost his grip on the sword and it fell to the ground.

'Oh no!' squealed Starlight.

'Watch out!' shouted Dad.

'Yikes!' cried Redwon.

Too late. The Purple Knight was on him, gripping his arm and pressing him against the tree trunk.

'What now, Redwon?' he said and he pulled a knife from his velvet saddle bag (beautifully embroidered in gold thread by a local artist) and held it to our hero's throat. 'Tell me where the Jewels of Jaybal are – or you die.'

Refusing to spill the beans was a dangerous ploy and the Knight pressed the blade deeper

138

into Redwon's neck. Suddenly everything went black and he knew that this was the end.

Luckily for Redwon, it was only the end for the Purple Knight. The rope the hero had been trying to cut suddenly snapped and the cage, Dad and Starlight dropped and landed on top of him. Good landing for them. Bad for the Knight.

'That is the second time you have saved my life, Superhero,' said Dad. 'But won't you tell me your name?'

'Oh, yes. Pweeeeese,' said Starlight. 'Tell uth! Tell uth! Tell uth!'

Then, to their surprise, Redwon flung off his cloak and his helmet. Dad and Starlight stood there, looking at him in astonishment.

'It's me, Watt,' he said.

'What?' said Dad.

'What?' said Starlight.

'Yes, that's right,' he replied. 'I have destroyed our enemies and now I will take you home.'

They were all amazed and overjoyed.

'I can't wait to thee our dear little houth again,' said Starlight. 'But what about dear old Gwandol?'

Grandol was sitting on the ground, still out of breath and looking pathetic in a sentimental-old-grandfather kind of way.

'Come home with us, Grandol,' said Watt. 'We will take care of you.'

As he couldn't speak, he just nodded gratefully into his beard.

They all went back to their cottage. The girl in the supermarket (with the blonde hair and the blue eyes) came to live with them and did the cooking and stuff. No more mushroom soup.

Best of all, when Redwon had managed to sell the Jewels of Jaybal on the Internet, they bought the Purple Knight's castle for a song and – after they'd redecorated – they lived happily ever after.

## THE END

*Max's novel eventually won the Whitcake Award for Children's Books and sold almost as many copies as Harry Potter.*